Something was wrong, desperately wrong. She was scared to death she was losing the man she loved.

"I know something's troubling you, Parnell, and I want to help, whatever it is. But you've got to tell me what's happening. I can't go on like this."

He stopped, but wouldn't look her in the eye. She reached out and touched his arm. He flinched. Hurt, she withdrew her hand as quickly as if she'd touched hot coals. When he refused to face her, she walked around in front of him.

"Why are you shutting me out?"

"I'm not shutting you out. I just need time." He looked up, stared at her, pure misery in his eyes. He stood as straight, as rigid and aloof, as the nearby lamppost. Brenda could see his frustration as he clenched and unclenched his gloved hands.

"How long do you need, Parnell? Forever? Because, let me tell you, that's what it feels like!"

She waited, throat tightening. She studied him in the light of the street lamp. The lines etched across the planes of his face seemed to have deepened, as if they'd been cut by a master hand. Lines of pain, of struggle. She ached for him, but she couldn't reach him.

"What's wrong?" she said at last. "I want to be with you, whatever you're going through. For better or worse. I'm going to be your wife, after all."

He closed his eyes and hauled in a ragged breath. Then he looked at her, spreading his hands in a helpless gesture. "That's just it. I don't know how to explain. . .but things have changed for me. . ."

UNA MCMANUS was born in Dublin, Ireland, and came to the United States nearly twenty years ago. Una makes her home in Columbia, Maryland, with her Pennsylvania Dutch husband and their three strapping sons. She enjoys telling earthly stories about divine love because the greatest Teacher of all was a storyteller. She formerly wrote for **Heartsong Presents** as Elizabeth Murphy.

Books by Una McManus (Elizabeth Murphy)

HEARTSONG PRESENTS
HP125—Love's Tender Gift
HP138—Abiding Love
HP154—Tender Mercy

Abide
With Me

Una McManus

Heartsong Presents

To Mark Littleton and Peggy Hart. Thank you
for reading my ramblings.

To Katherine Doster of the C.S. Lewis Insti-
tute. Thank you for your dog stories.

A note from the Author:
*I love to hear from my readers! You may write to me at
the following address:*   **Una McManus**
                              Author Relations
                              P.O. Box 719
                              Uhrichsville, OH 44683

ISBN 1-55748-916-5

ABIDE WITH ME

Cover illustration by Jean Brandt.

PRINTED IN THE U.S.A.

one

"Brenda, you can't be serious! Haven't you told him yet?"

Brenda Rafferty slapped the label on her mother's prescription and glanced uneasily across the pharmacy counter. "No, not yet."

"Your wedding. . .why, Valentine's Day is only ten weeks away. Darling, you can't keep something like this from your fiancé."

Brenda sighed. She knew her mother, a respected Christian counselor, was right. But Brenda felt she was being dragged kicking and screaming through a door she didn't want to enter. "Mom, I'll tell Parnell in my own way, in my own time."

"Oh, you always were my stubborn one," Louise Ford chided, reaching across the white Formica to pat her youngest daughter's hand.

"Mother, please! I don't need to be reminded of that particular character flaw!"

"Sorry, darling. I meant no offense. Stubbornness can be good or bad, depending upon how you use it. But my point is, don't wait too long to tell Parnell, or he may end up finding out some other way. I'd hate to see you hurt again."

Brenda shook her head, feeling the weight of her heavy blond hair bob against her shoulders. "Oh, Mom, don't be silly. That episode's so far in my past, how could he possibly find out unless I tell him?"

"You never know, darling. Secrets have a way of coming to light, especially when we're trying to hide them from our mate . . .or future mate."

"I'm not hiding anything from Parnell, Mom." Suddenly Brenda felt like a cantankerous teen instead of a twenty-nine-year-old pharmacist, once widowed and now about to marry again and become stepmother to a six-year-old boy. Why was she feeling resentment toward her mother? Why this guilt and fear in the

5

face of so much happiness?

"I'm just. . .delaying, until the right time. Anyway, Mom, some women keep this kind of thing private forever."

"I know, but secrets can be like time bombs." Louise Ford arched a well-groomed eyebrow. "Believe me, I've seen them explode. I'm counseling a couple right now who are separating because the wife felt so betrayed when she discovered a secret her husband had been keeping from her for ten years! Now the wife says she can't live with a man she can't trust. Darling, I don't want to see something like that happen to you. Marriages must be built on honesty and trust, right from the beginning. Secrets destroy trust."

Brenda nodded and handed Mrs. Ford a small brown paper bag containing her arthritis medication. She wished her mother hadn't brought up the subject. *Why not let sleeping dogs lie? At least until I'm not so busy.* With two dozen prescriptions to fill before noon and weeks of Christmas rush, the last thing Brenda needed was to agonize over how to tell Parnell the whole truth.

Her mother slipped the paper bag into her burgundy leather purse and checked her watch. "Oh my, if I don't rush, I'll be late for my eleven o'clock!" Even at fifty-five, Louise Ford's beauty was still striking; her face had the classic Grace Kelly look, framed by elegantly coiffed golden hair. "Just think about what I've said, honey. Parnell loves you. He'll understand. Better tell him before Christmas."

Brenda thrust her hands into the pockets of her white pharmacy coat, willing all her tension into her clenched fists. Everyone told her that with her china blue eyes, long, dark lashes, and slender, blond elegance, Brenda Ford Rafferty was a younger version of her mother. "I appreciate your concern, Mom, and I'll take your advice to heart. I'll think about it. I promise."

"That's my girl. It'll take courage, I know, but God will give you grace. And don't forget your dad and I are behind you."

Brenda smiled as her mother patted her hand again. "Dinner tonight?" Louise asked brightly.

"Not tonight. Parnell's taking me to the Inner Harbor in Baltimore. Says he's found a romantic little seafood shanty."

"Ah, yes, our Parnell is a real romantic, isn't he?" Louise motioned to the cut-glass vase of dark red roses on the counter. "Roses . . .again?"

"Again!" Brenda smiled. During their three-month engagement, Parnell Pierce had proven himself unflaggingly attentive. Flowers, candlelight dinners, surprise gifts. Brenda felt a rush of tenderness toward this sensitive man hidden behind the successful land developer.

Who would have thought? The first time they'd met, in this very room—Parnell owned the building that housed Brenda's pharmacy—he'd nearly frozen her out because of her Christian convictions. Back then, a cynical Parnell Pierce had no use for a God who would allow his family's lives to be taken in a senseless auto accident.   Parnell's mother, father, and wife had been on their way to the mall to buy Parnell a birthday present when rocks thrown by hooligans from the overpass had smashed into Fergus Pierce's windshield, causing him to lose control of his car, careen across the median, and plow into a speeding eighteen-wheeler.

In that one, fateful evening, Parnell had lost his entire family, except for his young son who'd stayed at home with him, and an ancient, senile grandmother confined to a nursing home in another state. He'd also abandoned his faith. But pain proved to be God's megaphone and, given time and much prayer on the part of Brenda and others, Parnell had surrendered his losses to God and moved into deeper levels of faith.

Yes, Parnell Pierce had come a long, long way from the brooding, unhappy man she'd first met, Brenda thought as she ran her mother's credit card through the machine. His suffering had given him a Christlike compassion for others, a strong commitment to the gospel, and a tender devotion to her that had won her heart against tremendous odds.

"Red for true love?" asked her mom, breaking in to Brenda's thoughts. She motioned to the roses on the counter.

"You got it. He even picks the most romantic color, as if getting married on Valentine's Day weren't enough!" Brenda pushed the charge slip toward her mother for her signature.

"Trust your Romeo with all your heart, darling." Louise Ford signed the slip with her usual flowing script, then buttoned her sky-blue London Fog raincoat against the Maryland cold. "He'll be dropping by soon, won't he?"

"Yes—and I don't want him to walk in on this conversation. So, scoot!"

"Message received." Louise Ford touched her fingers to her brow in a little salute and walked to the door, her black patent leather pumps clicking smartly against the gleaming white floor. She gave a small wave as she pushed open the swinging glass doors and disappeared into the cavernous marbled lobby of Thunder Hill Medical Center.

"Bye, Mom!"

Brenda pushed back her hair as she turned her attention to the pile of prescriptions, but her peace of mind had been shattered. Worry began gnawing at her. *I don't have time to think about this now*, she told herself sternly. *I'll figure out how to tell him . . .later.* She snatched a prescription off the top of the stack and began to count out an elderly man's heart medication.

But with the plonk of each pill hitting the bottom of the plastic container, doubts needled her like a toothache that wouldn't go away. *Will Parnell understand? Can I trust him to accept the worst about me?* A prickle of fear ran down her spine. *What if I lay everything on the line, and he pushes me away? What then?*

Plonk. Plonk. Plonk.

Don't be ridiculous Brenda. This is paranoia. Parnell is a committed Christian man who's about to become a committed Christian husband. Of course you can trust him.

The door swung open. Brenda's gaze shot up. Parnell stood in the open doorway, filling it, his presence suddenly dominating her otherwise empty store. Her first impressions were of raven black hair, a navy business suit, and vivid red roses. With his lean, angular frame and trimmed black beard, Parnell gave fresh meaning to the old cliche "tall dark, and handsome." His tanned face creased into a quixotic smile that emphasized the deep lines carving his face and adding a sophisticated maturity to his thirty-six years. He reminded Brenda of Clark Gable in *Gone with the Wind.* Her heart gave a lurch.

In several long strides Parnell was beside her, and Brenda found herself swept into his arms. She clung to him, surrendering to the comforting manliness of him, allowing herself to sink into the security of his embrace as a weary body snuggles into a thick down comforter. Her fears dissolved. His kiss took her to a place far beyond worries and deep, dark secrets—a place she never wanted to leave.

But reality impinged, as it always did. Brenda suddenly remembered prescriptions to be filled, phone calls to be returned, customers who could saunter through the door at any moment and be scandalized at the sight of their level-headed pharmacist caught in a passionate embrace.

"Parnell," she said, a little breathlessly, as she put her hands against his chest and tried to push him away. "How can a woman run a business with this carrying on?"

With a deep, rumbling chuckle, he scooped her off her feet and kissed her again, more playfully this time. Then he released her and grasped her hands. "Every time I see you, I fall in love all over again."

"Oh, you!" She smiled and inclined her head to sniff his newest bouquet of roses. She could tell Parnell was in an exceptionally good mood today. "They're beautiful, Parnell, but, really, you shouldn't buy me roses so often. It's too. . .extravagant! Besides, you might spoil me!"

Parnell traced her jawbone with his forefinger. "Oh, let me spoil you a little. These are weeds compared to your beauty," he whispered. "Anyway, I'm keeping the florist in business and contributing to the gross national product."

Brenda searched his brown eyes, feeling herself drown in their dark fire. *Oh, Parnell, would I be beautiful if you knew everything?* A deep sigh escaped before she could stop it.

"Brenda, what's wrong?" His jet-black brows drew together in a furrow of concern.

She blinked and smiled again. "Nothing. I just can't believe my happiness." *Well, that's not exactly a lie, but it is only half the truth. I can't believe how scared I am about telling you.*

"Believe it, my love."

Parnell stepped back, grabbed up the vase of faded roses and made his way to the small kitchenette nestled at the back of the shop.

"You don't need to do that, Parnell."

"But I want to," he called over his shoulder as he disappeared into the kitchenette.

ða

Parnell Pierce was a man who liked to do little things for his lady, and he wasn't ashamed to admit it. He hummed to himself as he bundled the old flowers into the trash, then dumped the stale water down the sink. Brenda was the ray of light that had shone into the darkness of his broken existence. Everything about his fiancée radiated life for Parnell, from the airy brightness of her pharmacy, with its ferns in brass pots and soft yellow walls that lured the sun inside, to the way her face lit up when she first saw him.

To Parnell, Brenda was all golds and pinks, with eyes blue as cornflowers. Her finely chiseled features went beyond physical loveliness. She possessed beauty of spirit, the generous gentleness praised in the Scriptures. But Brenda Rafferty was no pushover, Parnell reminded himself. He'd observed her strength of character when she stood up for her convictions. He shook his head as he remembered her unshakable faith in the face of his hostility toward God in the aftermath of the car accident.

Parnell turned on the faucet and filled the vase with water. In times past, before tragedy came calling, he'd ignored Christ, the living water his parents had tried so hard to pass onto him. Even though he'd been raised a preacher's kid, Parnell had never reached out to make that faith his own. But that had begun to change a year ago, when Brenda Rafferty rented space in his medical center.

He shut off the water, grimacing at the thought of the grudge he'd nursed against God for allowing his wife, Serena, to die.

He'd hardened his heart until he'd found himself backed into a corner, forced to admit the meaninglessness of life without God. Then Brenda had come into his bleak world and seen past the wall of cynicism he'd built around himself. Through her, he'd learned how to meet adversity with a sturdy faith and hope.

For months, Parnell had watched her endure cruel harassment aimed at driving her out of business—hate graffiti defacing her store, threatening phone calls, a war of nerves inflicted by some unknown assailant. She'd born up under the stress by clinging to her belief in a good God who would not abandon her, no matter what. Her spiritual steadfastness had made a deep impression on Parnell, prompting him to make his own leap of faith.

Now that Gil Montgomery had been revealed as Brenda's persecutor, Parnell would walk over coals before he'd see his lady hurt again by this fiend in five-hundred-dollar suits. Gil Montgomery. Even the man's name made his adrenaline pump. Parnell breathed deeply, trying to subdue his anger at the crooked senator's son, and prayed that he could release the situation to God. The law would take care of Montgomery; Parnell would take care of Brenda.

Ever since he'd walked into the pharmacy today, though, he had sensed something was bothering her. He assumed Montgomery's upcoming trial had put her on edge. Well, that rat's days as a free man were numbered. In the meantime, these flowers might distract her. At least, that was what Parnell hoped as he dropped the stems loosely into the vase. He wasn't much of a flower arranger, but he didn't need to be. The dark roses, deep greenery, and sparkle of cut glass shone with a clear, innocent beauty of their own.

"Brenda, I hope the news of Montgomery's trial hasn't upset you too much," Parnell said as he carried the arrangement of velvety roses into the pharmacy and placed it next to the cash register. He wanted the world, or at least the town of Columbia, to know he loved Brenda Rafferty. But, even more than that, he wanted to protect his woman from the ruthless man who'd tried to destroy her.

Brenda prickled at the name of her former business rival. Her hands tightened around the bottle of children's cough syrup she was filling. She knew she should love her enemies, but the mention of this man's name still rankled her. When graffiti and threats hadn't driven her out of town, he'd tampered with the labels on her drugs. Because of him, she'd nearly dispensed a lethal prescription!

Gil Montgomery, owner of a chain of drug stores, had attempted to sabotage Brenda's new business, largely because she was offering a unique service—compounding—that threatened his own profitability, she figured. By compounding medicines from scratch—something like baking a cake from scratch—Brenda could fill specialized prescriptions. Unusual medicines or drugs in unusually small quantities that drug companies didn't produce because of cost or short shelf-life. But compounding required licensing and specialized professional training, and the financial payoff wasn't great, although the emotional and spiritual satisfaction was. Brenda saw compounding as part of her Christian commitment to help people in need.

She was the first—and, so far—the only compounding pharmacist in Columbia. Montgomery had been consumed with jealousy when she arrived in town. Licensing himself and his pharmacists in compounding would have cost him time and money, and the bottom line wasn't lucrative enough to suit him. But compounding did draw many of his customers to Brenda's establishment, and that didn't sit well with Montgomery either. Apparently he didn't care who he mowed down to protect his profits, and so he'd tried to put her out of business. Now his trial was coming up.

Brenda looked up and saw the compassion softening Parnell's rugged features. "I'm dreading it. Absolutely dreading it."

"Have you been notified to testify yet?"

Brenda sighed. "Yes, I'm afraid so."

Parnell slipped his hand around her waist protectively. "Montgomery can't hurt you anymore, my love," he said, bending to kiss her forehead. "He'll have his day in court, but with Detective Lewis's evidence, it'll be an open-and-shut case. Over before it hits the papers."

Brenda glanced up into Parnell's face. The pale wintry light cast shadows, making the rugged lines around his eyes appear deeper. She drew comfort from his presence and his assurance. Yes, it would probably be over quickly. "The prosecutor says he'll call me in soon," she said.

Parnell's grip tightened. "Brenda, you're the most courageous woman I know. You'll do fine. And I'll be with you every step of the way."

She smiled and tried to swallow her apprehension. But her worries went deeper than just the court appearance. Parnell would always be there for her, wouldn't he? Even after he knew everything. . .

Don't wait too long. Secrets have a way of coming to light. Her mother's grim warning echoed in her mind like the incessant trilling of an alarm clock. She'd tell him tonight, over a plate of crabs at the Baltimore Inner Harbor. Her heart pounded at the thought. *Oh, Brenda, quit being such a coward. It'll be all right. Anticipation is the worst part, just like going to the dentist.*

Right. Telling him the whole truth would be no worse than a . . .root canal?

She straightened her shoulders and gently pulled away. "Parnell Pierce, would you let me get back to work before I can't afford to pay my rent?"

"Think I'd evict my favorite tenant?"

"Sure. . .in the blink of a fast-acting antibiotic."

"Hmm. The woman doesn't trust me." Parnell slid his hands down her arms without releasing her from his embrace. "I'll drop by your house. About six?"

"Perfect." Maybe everything would be perfect. She'd have to hang on to that thought.

"Wait a minute." He paused. "I have to drop off some donated toys at the Salvation Army. Can we make it 5:30?"

"OK, OK, but go now so I can get my work done!"

Parnell made another attempt to pull her closer. "Have I told you lately how adorable you look in that white pharmacy coat?"

"No! And I don't have time for sweet nothings right now." Brenda turned her head just in time to avoid his kiss. His lips brushed her cheek. She truly loved this playful side of Parnell—but she did have a pile of prescriptions waiting.

"Hard-hearted woman." He sighed, sliding his hands down her arms until he clasped her hands. Almost reverently, he raised her right hand to his lips. His mustache and beard felt soft against her skin, sending a tingle shimmering down her arm, raising goose bumps. "I love you, Brenda," he whispered. Then, he was gone.

Brenda stared after his long, muscular frame as he loped up the stairs toward his office on the fourth floor. A successful land developer, Parnell Pierce owned this building and scores of housing developments in and around Columbia. The energy he devoted both to his business ventures and to their relationship seemed practically boundless.

As boundless as his love for her. Would revealing her secret change that?

She closed her eyes. Her hands gripped the curved edge of the counter top. It felt cool and smooth to her touch. Her breath caught in her throat as she inhaled the heavy, sweet scent of roses.

Dear God, let him love me still. . .afterward.

❧

Business moved slowly for the rest of the day. A couple of rush prescriptions for patients in the hospital next door. A grandmother desperate for something to relieve her grandson's teething pain. A middle-aged businessman in need of Spandex knee supports to facilitate his newly acquired enthusiasm for jogging.

As usual, Brenda threw herself wholeheartedly into her work, striving to put the Golden Rule into practice by serving her customers as thoroughly and kindly as possible.

"Dr. Morrow, hello," she greeted a walk-in customer. "I noticed you just opened a practice in the basement." She took the middle-aged doctor's prescription, determined to handle it right away. She always tried to give the professionals in the building top priority.

"Yes, I have. Seems there can never be too many OB/GYNs."

Brenda darted a glance at the large, sandy-haired man who sported a walrus mustache the color of straw. Briefly, she wondered if Preston Morrow had played football during his undergraduate days.

"And I'm glad to see you do compounding," he continued, his accent betraying a Brooklyn upbringing. "I'll be needing your services for certain specialized medications."

Brenda scanned the prescription and her heart sank. Abiding by her Christian convictions sometimes brought its difficult moments, and this was one of them. "Uh, Dr. Morrow, I'm afraid we've got a problem here."

"Problem? What do you mean?"

She gazed into the doctor's frowning face and mustered her courage. "Dr. Morrow, as the pharmacist in this medical center, I'm committed to serving each doctor and patient as professionally as possible, but. . ."

"But?" His pale eyes narrowed.

"But it's against my personal code of ethics to dispense abortifacients. My training tells me these hormonal suppositories will be used to induce early abortions."

Morrow stood with his hands on his hips, his sandy brows furrowing. "What? You're telling me you won't fill this prescription?"

Brenda faced him squarely. Her heart was hammering, but she wasn't about to back down, not even for an angry man twice her size and age. "That's right, Dr. Morrow. I'd be happy to serve your other pharmaceutical needs, but not this one. It's a matter of conscience. I hope you can accept that." She handed him back the square slip of paper.

Morrow's face darkened. He tugged at his mustache. "What's it to you what a woman chooses to do with her body? Abortion is a protected legal right. It's a woman's private decision. We've left the Dark Ages behind, in case you hadn't noticed. Anyway, only a few of my patients require this procedure."

Brenda sighed. She knew all the arguments in favor of abortion, inside out, but she also knew how difficult it was to convince an abortionist of the sanctity of life. She glanced over at the play area beside the glass wall overlooking the tree-studded parking lot outside. A young mother sat on the window seat, cradling her sleeping infant. From the sturdy tan leather boots, faded blue jeans, and oversized flannel shirt so popular with high-school seniors, Brenda surmised the woman couldn't be more than seventeen.

Brenda looked from the girl back to Dr. Morrow. The doctor glowered, visibly irritated, tapping one fine Italian leather shoe against the floor, his arms crossed over his white professional coat. "So I've got to take my business across town, is that it? Some convenience having a pharmacist in the building who can't perform her duties because of a queasy conscience!"

Brenda controlled her impulse to blink and looked the man straight in the eye. "Dr. Morrow, what is legal is not necessarily what is moral. God is the Author of life; abortion is the taking of that life."

"Just my luck to land in your building," Morrow said loudly. "But mark my words, from now on, I'll take my business to Montgomery Drugs. And I can assure you, Mrs. Rafferty, I'll instruct my patients to avoid your bigoted, anti-woman establishment."

"I'm sorry you feel that way," Brenda said, careful to keep her voice even and reasonable. She didn't break eye contact with the doctor, but there was something menacing about his gaze that gave her chills. "Have you thought about what you're doing, Dr. Morrow? A woman has legitimate rights over her own body, to be sure, but she does not have the right to end the life growing inside her body."

Morrow cleared his throat and tugged at his mustache again. "Merely religious speculation. No one knows when life begins. Even theologians don't agree."

Brenda drew a deep breath. "That may be, Dr. Morrow, but abortion isn't only a matter of religion. Just because the Bible says 'Thou shalt not steal,' doesn't make embezzlement a religious issue. There are certain activities civilized people just don't accept. It doesn't take a religious person to say it's wrong to kill a child any more than to say it's wrong to steal money."

Morrow glared at her. "Mrs. Rafferty, I'm doing these women a much-needed service."

There was a sudden flurry of activity over by the window. "Now, just a minute!" In a swirl of red flannel and thick red hair, the young mother barreled toward them, babe in arms. Her freckled pixie face was flushed with anger. "I'm sick to death of that lie!"

Morrow raised a bushy eyebrow. "And what lie might that be, young lady?"

"Abortion does not serve women!" The girl pinned the doctor with her fierce gaze as she squared off against him. "It serves men who want easy sex. It serves doctors who make money off desperate women. But it does not serve women and children."

"Eh, Mrs. . ." Morrow began. His eyes flashed, narrowed. Brenda could see the veins in his thick neck bulging.

"It's Ellen Ruminski, and I'm not married," the young woman snapped, pulling her sleeping infant closer.

"Miss Ruminski, then, this is a professional discussion, of no concern to you."

"That's where you're wrong. Dead wrong. If I'd listened to someone like you, Molly would never have been born."

"Yes, well. . ." Morrow began to turn away.

"Look at her, doctor." Ellen turned the baby's peaceful face forward. "She's not just a blob of tissue to be disposed of. She's a real human being, every bit as alive as you or I. I thank God every day I listened to that prolifer outside the abortion clinic, or I would have killed. . .my own child." Her voice suddenly began to crack and she dashed a tear from her cheek. "Doctor, an abortion may kill a woman's baby, but it doesn't kill her motherhood. If I'd had an abortion, I'd still have been a mother—just the mother of a dead baby!"

"Ahem. . .yes. Well, as I said, abortion is a very personal choice. A choice I intend to continue to make available." With that, the bulky, white-coated doctor turned on his heel and stalked through the glass doors.

Brenda watched as he stood at the elevator, stabbing at the buttons. She found herself praying for him and for the women who were his patients.

And for the babies who would never belong to anyone—except God.

Ellen Ruminski looked at Brenda through long, reddish lashes and tucked a curl behind her ear. "I'm sorry I made a scene," she said. "But I had to say something."

"I'm glad you did. Your evidence is irrefutable." Brenda smiled at the baby who was beginning to stir. "God will bless you for doing the right thing and not taking the so-called easy way out."

"And God bless you for doing the right thing, too," Ellen said, turning her attention to her baby. "There, there, Molly," she crooned. "Go back to sleep. Sorry for the ruckus."

Brenda listened to the young mother coo to her child all the way back to the window seat. She marveled at how the whimper of a baby could transform a lioness into a kitten—and vice versa.

Frowning, Brenda quickly got back to her work. *So you think I did the right thing? If only you knew.*

two

"Let me get that, Brenda." Parnell reached for the large cardboard box crammed with toys and hefted it out of her arms. His breath frosted in the cold air.

She leaned back against Parnell's green Jaguar, which she jokingly referred to as his big-boy-toy, and clapped her hands to warm them. "What's in those boxes, anyway? Bricks?"

Parnell chuckled as he set the box down on the pavement next to the other two he'd just unloaded. He paused to button his gray wool overcoat. "People donated a lot of heavy stuff this year— books, electronic games, sports equipment, kiddie computers... that kind of thing."

"Did you put the donation boxes in all your buildings, or just the residential ones?"

A couple of trucks rumbled by on the downtown Baltimore street as Parnell bent over the open trunk to retrieve the last box. "Both. Actually, my business tenants gave the most."

"You came up with a neat idea."

Parnell stacked the last box on top of the others and gave a thumbs-up signal to the two Salvation Army youths manning the Christmas toy collection. "That's all till next week, guys."

The boys thanked him profusely. Brenda noticed that Parnell just nodded and quickly walked around to the driver's side of the car. This wasn't the first time Brenda had seen him duck adulation. Parnell was a man who liked to work behind the scenes, giving his alms in secret. She liked that.

"You know, Brenda, a lot of people really want to do good," he said, continuing their conversation across the roof of the car, raising his voice above the noise of passing traffic. "They just need someone to make the actual deeds a little more convenient for

19

their busy lives."

"Right." Brenda dug into her purse, fishing out a twenty-dollar bill. "Tell me about busy. I haven't even taken time to give money to the Salvation Army yet. And for me, Christmas doesn't start until I do."

She stuffed the bill into the bell ringer's kettle, wished a blessed Christmas to the young female officer, and climbed into the car beside Parnell. She was just reaching for her seat belt when he leaned over and grazed his lips against her cheek. Her eyes widened. "What's that for?"

"For one of the many things I love about you."

"Which one?" Her lips curved in delight.

"That you feel so compelled to give money to the Salvation Army at Christmas."

"It was a few bucks, Parnell. No big deal." She knew Parnell gave thousands to missionary work every month, but she wasn't about to mention that.

"It's the compulsion that counts, my love."

Brenda threw back her head and laughed, giddy with happiness. The way Parnell noticed things about her made her feel special and loved, and she told him so in no uncertain terms.

He grinned in reply. "Everything about you is important to me, Brenda. I'm crazy about you. Can't a man be crazy about the woman he's about to marry?"

He gazed at her with piercing tenderness. Brenda felt her stomach flip and her laughter trailed off. "Yes," she whispered, her voice thick with emotion.

☙

The lonely cry of seagulls keened over the dark water. Tiny shards of icy rain pattered against the glass separating Brenda from the Baltimore Harbor. Outside, the cold, calm waters reflected the December night sky. Inside, by candlelight, she watched Parnell's reflection in the window. He thrust a hand through his shock of coal black hair as he studied the gilt-edged menu. Knowing his gestures so well gave her a satisfying sense of intimacy. Love for him washed over her.

The newest seafood restaurant on the harbor was quaint and charming, with its polished woods, authentic fish netting, and antique brass lamps. Brenda savored the woodsy smell of the roaring fire, the gleam of fine silverware, and the hauntingly lovely melodies of the piano player. It felt good to be in such a beautiful place with the man she loved.

How infinitely merciful God was to bless her with this kind of love! After Mark died five years ago, she'd never expected to have these feelings again. But she'd found that with God—just as He promised—all things were possible. Watching Parnell, his dark, handsome looks set off by his tan tweed sports jacket and cream turtleneck, Brenda breathed a silent prayer of thanksgiving. Tonight there were no shadows across her heart.

At least, not yet. Perhaps she shouldn't risk breaking the mood by telling him tonight. Perhaps her mother was just being overly cautious. . .

Parnell looked up from the menu and smiled. "See anything you like?"

"You." Brenda reached across the linen, rose-colored tablecloth and entwined her fingers with his.

"I mean the food, silly."

"Oh, well, in that case," she laughed gaily, "the Parisian de la Mer sounds intriguing."

"Two Parisians it is, then," he said, signaling to the tuxedoed waiter. "Preceded by your favorite. . ."

". . .shrimp cocktail," she finished his sentence. "Don't I have any secrets left to surprise you with, Parnell Pierce?"

"It mystifies me why you agreed to marry me at all."

"Maybe it's your ability to choose restaurants," she said with a grin. "Or maybe it's all those roses and love letters and Godiva chocolates—so many that my wedding dress is going to have to be let out!" Brenda giggled, feeling as carefree as a careening seagull skimming the waves.

"You sound happy," he said, cupping one side of her face with his open palm. "I want to make you happy, Brenda, God knows."

"As I want to make you happy." She leaned into the softness of his flesh, inclined her head slightly, and kissed the palm of his hand. "I love you," she added in a whisper.

"I know you do," he whispered back, his voice low and husky, "my golden-haired princess."

"Er. . .excuse me. . .your appetizers." The stiff young waiter stood by their table, silver tray held shoulder high. "If you're ready. . .?"

Brenda blushed furiously and busied herself with her napkin. The round silver goblet was set before her, brimming with pink-veined shrimp nestled on a bed of fresh green lettuce. Rivulets of condensation ran down the chilled bowl.

The waiter served Parnell and refilled their glasses with iced tea. Then he nodded and slipped away into one of the other small dining rooms dotting the busy, rambling restaurant. After Parnell said a brief blessing, Brenda drove her heavy silver fork into the largest of the shrimp.

"Mmm, I didn't realize how hungry I was," she said between mouthfuls.

"Umm. . .me, too."

One course later, Brenda was delighted to discover Parisian de la Mer was tender scallops smothered in a rich, creamy basil sauce. "This is delicious, Parnell."

"I wanted this evening to be perfect. . .like you."

Brenda let the remark pass, but she shifted uneasily on her blue velvet chair. The pedestal Parnell sometimes put her on was an uncomfortable place to be. Deftly, she steered the conversation toward Parnell's son.

"How's Angelo's stomach? Any sign of irritation or ulcer? I notice I haven't refilled his medication recently."

Parnell unwrapped the foil covering his steaming baked potato. "I tell you, Brenda, having you in his life has done wonders for his digestion. Pity you can't bottle and dispense mother's love, or a soon-to-be stepmother's love, in this case."

"Stepmother!" Remembering all the wicked women of fairy-tale fame, she made a face. "Too bad Cinderella gave us such a bad name!"

"No problem." Parnell stirred a packet of sweetener into his tea. "Angelo doesn't think of you that way."

"I've prayed so much for the little guy to accept me. You know I've come to love him as if he were my own child."

Parnell stopped stirring. "Your own child," he echoed, giving her a probing look. "Have you thought about the children we may have?"

"Oh, I'll admit I've given it a thought or two." Brenda fought the blush she felt rising to her cheeks. "I wonder if they'll look like Black Beard the Pirate or Goldilocks."

Parnell smiled. "Both, I hope. I mean, I hope we have more than one. How about you? What size family do you want?"

Brenda paused, deep in thought as she sliced into a large scallop. "Well, I was brought up in a small family, and at times I found it lonely. So I like the idea of a large, happy family with huge Christmas dinners, filling up a whole pew at church. But. . ."

Parnell studied her face. "What's the problem then? You won't get any argument out of me. I'd love a passel of kids."

"Well, there's my career. . . ." Brenda cocked her head, her forkful of scallops stopping in midair. "I'm wondering how I can be both a prolific mother and a prolific pharmacist, if you know what I mean."

"I know exactly what you mean. Serena had a difficult pregnancy, and I saw the toll it took on her. And she wasn't even working full time. No, Brenda, even though I'd like a whole football team of kids, I'd never ask you to take on more than you could handle."

"So you've got nothing against working wives?"

"Not a thing. I just don't buy the line that wives who are also mothers can have everything at the same time."

Brenda put down her fork. "OK. Explain."

Parnell grinned, his white teeth remarkable against his black mustache. "A woman shouldn't have to feel she's got to be Superwoman, working long hours away from home and taking care of babies at the same time. I think it's extremely difficult for a mother to devote herself fully to her career when her children are little—not like she can when they're older."

Brenda nodded. "Go on. So far, I like what I'm hearing."

"I also think that many women feel pressured to prove them-
selves in the business world because our society has so devalued
motherhood. But raising the children God has entrusted to us is
the most important job most of us will ever do. Jesus Himself
described God as a heavenly Parent."

Brenda felt her admiration of Parnell swell. She clasped his
hand and squeezed it. "I'm so glad you feel that way. I want
children, but I also want to continue my career. I love my work,
you know."

"I could tell that from the first time I met you. I still remember
the pride in your voice when you showed me your compounding
equipment. How is business these days, anyway?"

"Really good," she said, releasing his hand and spearing a forkful
of artichoke, asparagus, and snow pea medley. "The Hospice
people now use me almost exclusively. I work with each dying
patient to see how I can best deliver pain medication. It's awesome to be able to relieve a person's pain so that he can enjoy his
last few hours with family and friends."

Parnell took a sip of iced tea. "It must be very satisfying. So
you can count on me to support you if you want to continue your
career, even after you become a mother to a whole football team!"

"Oh, you!" She swatted at him with her napkin. "Football
team, indeed!"

Parnell made a comical face. "Then how about six? Or four?"

Brenda chuckled and unwrapped a pat of butter for her baked
potato. "How about one or two, and then see how we feel? I
don't like planning every detail. No room left for God's little
surprises."

"Sounds good to me," replied Parnell in between mouthfuls.
"We'll have all the nannies and housekeepers it takes for you to
continue running the pharmacy. We can even hire another full-
time pharmacist so the shop will always be covered. Since I'm
my own boss, I can be involved with the daily details of the
children's lives. Field trips, volunteering at school. . ."

"Staying up all night with colicky babies?"

He grinned. "All night, so you can sleep. That's a promise."

"I'm going to hold you to that, buster!" Brenda chortled. "No wonder I love you," she added, growing serious. "Thank you for understanding how important my career is to me. It's more like a ministry than a job, you know."

"I know. I see how you talk to customers. People who go into your shop looking anxious, come out with a peaceful look on their faces."

"Running a pharmacy built on godly values has been my dream ever since I recommitted my life to Christ as a teenager." Brenda smiled, a little wistfully. "It was Mark's dream, too. . ."

She could feel Parnell's eyes on her. "Do you still miss him?"

Brenda thought about her late husband. "Yes, but there's no pain. Just gratitude for the years we had together."

"Brenda, you told me something once, back in my dark days: 'The Lord gives, the Lord takes away, and sometimes the Lord gives back again.' I wonder if you realize how much that one comment helped restore my faith and come to terms with my loss of Serena?"

The reminder of her grandmother's saying brought a smile to Brenda's lips. "I'd almost forgotten that little gem. Well, Grandma Ford certainly knew about loss. She lost her youngest child and her husband while she was still in her twenties."

"I'm glad I'm part of your dream, Brenda."

She glanced up at him through her lashes. "I'm glad you are, too. It's nice to know I have someone on my side. Sometimes sticking to one's values can be pretty lonely."

"Oh? What's up?"

"That new doctor in the basement, Dr. Morrow. . .he wanted me to dispense abortifacients."

Parnell's brows furrowed. "But he's an OB/GYN, isn't he? Not an abortionist."

"Yes, I know. But today he asked me to make up suppositories of hormones used to induce early abortions."

"That's legal?" Parnell's dark eyes widened.

Brenda shrugged. "There's no law against physicians doing these procedures in their offices. Of course, he claims abortions are only a small part of his practice."

"Oh, I see."

Brenda studied Parnell as he chewed thoughtfully. "Where do you stand on the abortion issue?" she asked after a moment's hesitation. Up until now, she'd assumed his Christian commitment would make it impossible for him to accept abortion as morally permissible. Now she realized she didn't know how he stood on the issue.

Parnell sliced into his baked potato and sprinkled on salt and pepper liberally. "I'm pro-choice, I guess. Since it's a woman's body, carrying a child has to be her decision. But, even so, I can't say I'm comfortable with abortions being performed in my building."

"Do you believe abortion is wrong?" she probed.

Parnell took another drink of tea. For a long moment, the only sound was the clink of ice against glass. "Well, the Scriptures seem to speak against it, but I feel it's up to each woman to wrestle with her own conscience. It's between her and God. After all, I can think of situations where abortion might be the lesser of two evils."

Brenda swallowed hard. "Such as?"

"Say, rape. Or incest. Or the age of the woman. Maybe a teenager, for example, shouldn't have to pay for one mistake for the rest of her life. After all, isn't God a God of mercy and grace?"

Brenda felt her stomach knot in disappointment. A hard, savage disappointment. This was such an important issue for her. She'd hoped for a strong prolife conviction on Parnell's part. It wasn't there. Mechanically, she chewed her food. The scallops, so tender and delicious only minutes ago, seemed to stick in her throat like splinters of dried driftwood. After a moment, she said quietly, "But, Parnell, mercy isn't always what's expedient or convenient at the moment."

"Uh huh." He looked at her through narrowed eyes. "But sometimes what's expedient is also what's necessary."

She took a deep breath. "With so many people wanting to adopt," she began tentatively, hopefully, "there's really no such thing as an unwanted child."

Parnell put down his glass. "Now that's something I find hard to identify with," he said, spearing a piece of steamed asparagus. "Adoption. How can a woman give up her own flesh and blood? I can't conceive of giving Angelo to strangers."

He spoke casually, almost off the cuff, but his words rattled Brenda like a gale-force wind, battering against her sensitive spirit. Miserably, she pushed her food around the plate. *This doesn't bode well for your little confession, Brenda. Not at all.* Despite the warmth of the restaurant, her blood suddenly ran as cold as the wintry water lapping the stone walls enclosing the harbor.

"What's the matter, Brenda? You're as pale as a ghost."

Now was the moment for total honesty, she realized. But her courage deserted her. She gave Parnell a weak smile and shrugged. "Nothing's the matter. I guess the confrontation with Dr. Morrow upset me more than I realized."

"Did you refuse to fill his order?"

"Yeah." Brenda could feel her heart thumping. The knot in her stomach threatened to dissolve into tears if she didn't keep a tight, tight rein on her emotions. She kept her gaze on her food so Parnell couldn't see her eyes. She wasn't ready to reveal that inner, wounded part of herself.

Not yet. Not as long as he felt this way.

"I'm glad you followed your conscience," Parnell said, reaching across the table and giving her hand a quick squeeze. "Like I said, you're the most courageous woman I know. I suppose Morrow will go to your competition."

"Oh, he made that quite clear. And he's going to send his patients to Montgomery Drugs as well." Suddenly tired, she pushed at her hair.

"So Gil Montgomery still profits!" Parnell said, bitterness creeping into his tone. "I hope they put him away for life after what he did to you."

Brenda warmed under Parnell's protectiveness. She found the

corners of her mouth tugging up into a tentative smile and exhaled the breath she didn't realize she'd been holding. Gradually some of her tension eased. She recalled how Parnell had helped her uncover the fingerprint evidence that had nailed Montgomery. How Parnell had comforted her after a drunken Montgomery had tried to force himself on her after their one disastrous dinner date. . .

Brenda shook her head, trying to shed the ugly memory. Parnell's hand tightened around hers. She focused on his face and saw anxiety, and she knew that anxiety was for her. Parnell had been a refuge then. She'd trust God to open his eyes to her view of the sacredness of life now. Perhaps then he'd understand her situation. . . Perhaps then she could tell him everything, share her heart with her beloved as she longed to do.

๛

The heart-stirring strains of Rachmaninoff's Second Symphony filled the leather and mahogany interior of Parnell's green Jaguar. The music rose and fell in great waves as he threaded through the night traffic on I-95 toward Columbia. Brenda relaxed into the soft leather seat. She closed her eyes and let the music sweep over her, swelling and diving like her own emotions. The events of the day had battered her more than she cared to admit.

Parnell glanced over at her, one hand on the steering wheel, as the powerful car purred down the expressway, cutting effortlessly through the night. "You OK?"

"Yes," she said, closing her heavy eyelids. "Just tired." *Well, that's not a lie. I'm weary of this secrecy. . .*

The warmth from the heater cosseted her and she dozed fitfully, drifting in and out of a discomforting dream. Parnell was walking away from her, disappearing into a swirling, gray fog. She ran after him, out of breath, heart hammering, crying that she was sorry, that she'd meant to tell him. But he ignored her pleas and kept on walking.

Suddenly, she found herself in her own driveway.

"Wake up, sleepyhead," Parnell said softly as he placed a kiss on her forehead. "You're home."

Brenda groaned groggily. In her murky, anguished state, she stretched up her arms to encircle Parnell, drawing him closer. She drank in the comfort of him like a dry flowerbed greedily soaking up a surprise rainstorm. He was here, with her. He hadn't walked away. She blinked her eyes open. The eerie light of the full moon spilled over him, cutting craggy lines into his face, accentuating the strong planes of his cheekbones and the ebony of his hair and beard.

Over his shoulder, her small, white Cape Cod glimmered in the moonlight, burnished with an ethereal timelessness. Parnell's presence seemed to seep into every nook and cranny of her being. Brenda's heart began to race as their awareness of each other ignited like dry twigs on a fire. His breath felt warm against her face. His raw masculinity kindled a response in her own blood. How easy it would be to give in to the comfort of physical intimacy. . .just this once.

Whoa, Brenda! Be careful! Don't play with fire or you'll get burned!

Immediately, she pulled back from him, bracing one hand against the buttery-soft leather seat. "I'd better go in," she said, her voice firm.

"Maybe that would be a good idea." Parnell let his arms drop. "Not that I want you to go. . ."

"I know. I know. But, to be honest, the longer I stay here alone with you, the harder it is to stick to our agreement—no physical intimacy before marriage. We're just asking for trouble."

Parnell arched a black eyebrow. "So now I'm trouble, huh?"

Brenda giggled a little. "As a matter of fact, yes. Actually, you're irresistible."

"Baby, am I glad to hear that!"

They laughed and exchanged a brief kiss. Suddenly, Parnell's mood turned serious. Gently, he pushed back the strands of golden hair that had escaped Brenda's hair clip and fell around her face. "Only two more months, my love," he said softly. "Then you'll be mine, to have and to hold, until death do us part. I can wait a little longer. After all, I only started living again when I started loving you."

Brenda felt a lump thickening in her throat. She placed her hand over his. "To have and to hold, body and soul. We can wait."

She gathered her purse and coat and stepped out of the car. Her blacktopped drive was slick from the recent rain, and Parnell waited until she'd walked safely to the porch and unlocked the door.

She turned and waved as he backed out of the driveway onto the empty street and drove away into the dark night. She stood on the porch, hand on the doorknob. She noticed she was trembling. Parnell was committed enough to Christ to defer his physical desires. Just as the book of Proverbs taught, he was a man with rule over his own spirit. She loved him for that.

Still, she couldn't help worrying. His weak stance on abortion and his lack of understanding regarding adoption bothered her more than she cared to admit, even to herself.

She shivered. How would he react when he knew the whole sad, ugly story?

It frightened Brenda to realize she didn't know.

three

"Look, Brenda, ducks. . .and swans!" Angelo Pierce squealed, his breath making wispy clouds in the chilly midday air.

The dark-haired, pint-sized version of his father, could hardly contain his excitement when he spotted a few lonely mallards and two bedraggled swans waddling alongside Lake Kittamaqundi, the huge, man-made mirror of a lake in downtown Columbia.

"How. . .uh. . .wonderful, honey." Brenda tried to inject more enthusiasm into her voice than she felt. In another second, Angelo would insist on traipsing across the muddy grass for a closer look. Brenda quickly slipped her arm around the small boy and guided him into the warm, fragrant interior of the Pizza Palace. Secretly, she felt sorry for the waterfowl with the long, cold winter ahead, but she didn't dare voice her concern. Angelo would want to take them home and probably make a case for tucking them into his bed.

Parnell's mansion just outside Columbia was already home to a host of Angelo's animal refugees: three box turtles, saved from certain death and possible dismemberment on Route 32; a couple of stray, mangy, and sullenly ungrateful cats; a runaway rabbit, blind in one eye (most likely an escapee from some other boy's cage); and a bright yellow canary that had had the good fortune to land on Parnell's deck after sustaining an injury to his wing. The bewildered bird had convalesced in Angelo's shoebox hospital for months. Now he filled the kitchen with his continuous high-pitched trilling, despite the complaints of Mrs. Crebs, Angelo's nanny. Yes, indeed, after a year of knowing Angelo Pierce, Brenda wasn't about to express sympathy for ducks. Or swans or geese or

31

any other bird or animal that could conceivably be carried home.

Inside the restaurant, Jim, a gangly young waiter with an acne-scarred face, greeted them. "Your usual booth?" Jim attended Howard Community College during the week, but on weekends, he wore the Pizza Palace uniform—black pants and red vest—and waited tables. Since this was Angelo's favorite eatery, Jim was like an old friend.

"Sure thing, Jim." Brenda grabbed Angelo's hand as she hurried to keep up with Jim's leggy strides, leading the way to the booths overlooking the lake.

"Pepperoni with extra cheese?" he asked as she and Angelo scooted in on the squeaky red vinyl seats. It was really more a statement than a question. They always ordered pepperoni with extra cheese. No deviations, no surprises. Angelo had a sense of adventure when it came to animals, but he clung to the tried and proven with his diet.

Brenda glanced at the small boy. He nodded, grinning.

"Right. The usual. Iced tea for me and apple juice for the young gentleman."

Angelo pulled a long face. "Aw, no juice! My tummy feels good now. I want Coke."

"Your stomach's really OK?" Angelo's ulcers seemed to be a thing of the past. Still, Brenda didn't like taking chances with his health.

"Yeah, it's great." After a second's reflection, he added emphatically, "For real!"

The earnestness on the small face brought a smile to Brenda's lips. "OK, Jim, you heard the man. Diet Coke."

Jim nodded, pocketed his notepad, and strode away, his legs eating up the distance to the kitchen.

Brenda slipped off her black wool coat and reached over the table to help Angelo struggle out of his quilted jacket. She'd taken him to soccer practice this Saturday morning, as she often did when Parnell put in extra time on one of his building projects—

his latest a senior housing development, designed for semi-communal living. Brenda was glad to have this one-on-one time with her future stepson.

"Do ya think our team will win?" Angelo asked, his face, still tanned from the summer, creased into a worried frown. Actually, his team was just turning the corner into a winning streak. Brenda was amazed at how well they played—for first-graders, at least.

"With you on the team, they can't lose."

Angelo broke into a grin. "Are you lying?"

"No, I most definitely am not lying!" Brenda chuckled at their shared joke. A year ago, when she had first met Angelo, the boy would have labeled any incorrect fact as a "lie." To his way of thinking, lying was anything that didn't accord with reality, such as making an error about the weather. The young truth-seeker immediately and vociferously branded any incorrect fact as a "lie." It had taken much explanation for him to grasp the difference between mistakes and deliberate falsehoods, and Brenda wasn't convinced he totally understood the concept yet. But she always found it interesting that he equated what was real with what was true.

Suddenly, as if from nowhere, an arrow of fear shot through her heart, poisoning her lighthearted mood. How would Angelo rate her secret? The reality of her situation was different from the way it looked. Would he think she was a "liar" for concealing the truth?

More importantly, would he be right?

Quickly, Brenda shoved the disturbing thoughts from her mind. When the time came for revelation, Angelo would understand. Of course he would. Just as Parnell would understand.

Why, then, was she so scared to tell them?

"Brend-a-a-a! Aren't you listening to me?"

Angelo's voice broke into her consciousness. She snapped back into the present and smiled at the little boy. "Sorry, I missed that. What did you say?"

Before he could tell her, Jim had returned with a huge, steaming pizza. With a couple of expert flicks of his round pizza cutter, he presented Brenda with the first slice. "Double pepperoni and double cheese," he announced.

The white topping oozed off the triangular slice in long gooey strings. Brenda inhaled deeply of the fragrant Italian herbs. "Ah!"

"Ah!" Angelo echoed, already angling his piece toward his mouth, imitating the motions and sounds of a train chugging toward a tunnel.

For several quiet minutes, they both satiated their appetite. After his second slice, Angelo abruptly resumed the conversation. "Kids at school say you can't be my mommy for real."

"Why not?" Puzzled, Brenda put her slice of pizza down and turned her full attention on the little face, smeared with tomatoey sauce.

"Because my real mommy died." He blinked back his tears.

Brenda reached across the black tabletop and cupped Angelo's hand. Even after two years, the youngster sometimes couldn't help crying when he talked about his mother or looked through old photograph albums showing her likeness. His sorrow was sometimes daunting, causing Brenda herself to wonder if she could ever fill that mother-shaped place in his heart. "It's OK to feel sad," she said softly, careful to respect his dignity. "I'd feel very, very sad if my mother died, you know."

"You would?"

"Sure. And I think you're very brave to open your heart to a new mommy."

"I am?" Angelo's chocolate-brown eyes grew wide.

"I can never take her place, Angelo. She'll always be your real mom, and that's how it should be. But I can be your second mommy, your stepmom. I think since Serena's in heaven now, she's happy that you get to have another mommy who loves you and wants to take good care of you."

Brenda could see that Angelo was thinking hard. His brow

furrowed, and he stared at his plate in solemn silence. Brenda's heart went out to him and she squeezed his hand. The bones felt so small, so fine. The boy's vulnerability called forth every atom of maternal protectiveness in Brenda's being. *This must be how God yearns to protect us, to gather us under His wing like a mother hen.*

"I promise, Angelo, I'll be the best stepmommy a boy ever had. See those ducks and swans?" She motioned toward the lake. "When winter comes, they won't leave the lake. Some birds, like the swallows, fly south for the winter. Not these guys. They stay home with their families. Just like I'm gonna stay with you."

A smile of relief spread across Angelo's face. "So you'll stay with me, just like the ducks?"

"You got it!"

Angelo's grin seemed to rival the dawn. "Promise? You'll be my stepmom forever?"

"Forever," she promised, sealing the deal with another squeeze of his hand. "But I do need to know one thing."

"Yeah?" Angelo's pizza came to a halt in midair.

"Why aren't you eating your crusts?" Brenda pointed to the small mountain of discarded pizza pieces balancing on the ede of Angelo's plate.

"Oh, they're for the ducks. They like pizza, too."

Brenda rolled her eyes. "I needn't have asked."

20

Tori Manning slammed down the newspaper on the pharmacy counter. "I can't believe it, Aunt Brenda! Just because Gil Montgomery is a senator's son and can afford a fleet of high-priced lawyers, does he think he can get away with almost poisoning someone?"

Brenda, in the process of preparing the ingredients to compound a bubble-gum-flavored cold remedy for a child, paused and glanced at the headlines her eighteen-year-old niece and part-time assistant found so offensive: MONTGOMERY PLEADS INNOCENT. Brenda sighed. "What else did we expect, Tor? That he'd admit his crime?"

Tori snorted, tossing her long brown hair over the shoulders of her white pharmacy coat. "Exactly! If he's guilty, he should admit it."

"Oh, Tori, if only we lived in a perfect world."

A smile crept from Tori's pretty mouth to her large hazel eyes. "Think I'm a starry-eyed idealist, that I'm expecting too much?"

"For this sinful world. . .yes."

"But. . .if his plan had succeeded—switching drugs like that— why, you could have killed Mrs. Phillips!" Tori shuddered. "I can't bear to think about it, Aunt Brenda."

Indeed, Brenda had come perilously close to dispensing a lethal dose of digitalis, a drug poisonous in anything over tiny amounts, instead of a nutritional supplement called chromium. Both substances resembled finely ground white powder, indistinguishable to the naked eye. Brenda herself didn't like to think how close she'd come to tragedy. "Just thank God I double-checked the label."

In his haste to reaffix the switched labels, Gil Montgomery had gotten them slightly askew, just crooked enough to arouse Brenda's suspicion. Ruining her professionally would have discredited her compounding service and removed Brenda as his business competitor.

"It was greed—pure greed—on his part," muttered Tori. She slipped the newspaper under the counter and fished out an elastic band from the pocket of her white coat. In one fluid motion, she gathered her brown hair into a thick, high-swinging ponytail that gave her the appearance of a carefree 1950s girl. Brenda often said all she needed was a poodle skirt and a soda fountain to complete the image. Quickly, Tori turned her atention to organiziang the pile of prescriptions waiting for Brenda. "He just didn't want to invest the time and money training himself and his pharmacists so they could offer compounding, too," she added.

"Well, compounding isn't a big moneymaker, you know. The training is expensive, and it take two years to get certified."

"All that guy cares about is making money!" Tori snorted, entering a prescription into the computer. "That's a lousy motive for a pharmacist, if you ask me. I thought this was a helping profession."

"I agree with you, Tor. But Gil told me once that he was building a financial empire, and for whatever reason, he saw me as a threat. I just wish this trial were over. I'm not looking forward to testifying and having Gil Montgomery glare at me."

"Don't worry, Aunt Brenda. I've got a Scripture verse for you."

Brenda couldn't help smiling. Her niece, despite her heavy academic load in the pre-pharmacy program at George Washington University, was an enthusiastic Bible student and always seemed to come up with just the right verse. "Preach it, sister."

" 'If God be for us, who can be against us?' Even on the witness stand." She flashed a smile and a wink.

"Very encouraging, Tor. And I have a verse for you."

The girl's eyebrows shot up, and she waited expectantly.

" 'Pray for those who hate you and persecute you.' "

Tori's face fell. "That's a tough one, Aunt Brenda. Pray for Gil Montgomery? After what he's done to you?" She pursed her lips.

"But that's what the Lord expects of us, Tor. Even if we have to ask for the grace to do it. We don't have to feel like forgiving him, we just have to want to."

Tori sighed and shrugged her shoulders. "OK, I know you're right. I still don't want to pray for that rat, but I'm willing to ask God to help me want to."

Brenda nodded and both women lapsed into companionable silence as they attended to their duties. Brenda filled prescriptions, praying for each patient, while Tori inventoried stock and served the occasional walk-in customer. Monday mornings were usually unhurried, the lull giving them a chance to catch up and prepare for the afternoon rush and the "changing of the guard" as

Tori called it. When she left for her university classes at four o'clock, Rita Andreas took over as Brenda's assistant.

Ever since Brenda Rafferty, then Brenda Ford, had recommitted her life to Christ after several rebellious teenage years, she'd dreamed of owning her own pharmacy, a business based on the Christian principles of service, love, and adherence to truth. In her early twenties, she'd shared that dream with her husand as they worked their way through pharmacy school. Five years ago, after Mark's death at the hands of a drunk driver, she'd taken the insurance money, gone to Texas to study compounding, and set up shop in Columbia, near her parents and her sister, Marcie Manning.

Gil Montgomery had not only tried to destroy her dream, but had also attempted to turn Brenda against Parnell. He'd actually made it look like Parnell Pierce was the one making the harassing phone calls and defacing Brenda's shop with anti-Christian graffiti. Because of Parnell's hostility toward God at the time, Brenda had suspected him for a while, but he had hung in there with her and eventually helped her gather the fingerprint evidence that had led to Montgomery's arrest.

Now she and Parnell were past all that. They could spend their energies nurturing their relationship and preparing for their life together as husband and wife, father and stepmother. At least, as soon as she testified and Gil Montgomery was convicted. After that, the whole incident would be nothing more than a bad memory. Over. Finished.

Gil Montgomery couldn't hurt her or Parnell anymore. . .could he?

❧

"Sorry I'm late!" Rita Andreas breezed into the pharmacy, her waist-length hair swirling around her petite frame like a black satin sheet.

Brenda glanced up from her work, checking a twinge of irritation at her assistant's tardiness. This was the third time this week.

Rita threw down her purse and pulled off her purple and yellow down jacket, jamming it onto the coat tree. "Honestly, Brenda, I am sorry. Another one of those long 'discussions' with Reggie, as he calls them. Arguments is more like it, if you ask me."

"Oh. . .Reggie." Brenda had met Rita's boyfriend when he'd stopped by the pharmacy to pick Rita up after work one day. There was an arrogance about him that Brenda didn't like. Reggie played guitar, and Rita spent every free evening at the Christian coffee house where he performed. At work, she mooned and sighed and fretted over him, more like an infatuated teen than her twenty years would indicate. Brenda attributed her assistant's immaturity to the fact that Rita's father had deserted his family.

"What I do for love!" Rita quoted dramatically as she slipped into her white coat and straightened her name tag. The younger woman didn't have a pharmacy degree—only a high-school education—so her duties revolved around ringing up sales, answering the phone, filing, stocking shelves, and dealing with customers. She was a natural with people, always cheerful and willing to listen to someone else's problems. The regular customers loved her.

Brenda smoothed out the label on the bottle she had just filled and glanced around the shop. Mercifully, the steady stream of customers seemed to have dried up temporarily. She studied Rita's face. Behind the theatrics and forced cheerfulness, Brenda saw pain. Rita could no more hide her feelings than she could hide the Cherokee ancestry in her sharp, high cheekbones, tan skin, and coal black eyes. "Want to talk about it? It's time for a cup of tea anyway."

"Thanks, Brenda. I could use both."

Over mugs of steaming herbal tea in the kitchenette off the back of the shop, Rita poured out her woes. It was the same old story Brenda had heard from young women in the youth group at church, the same old issues she herself had wrestled with.

"It always seems to come down to sex." Rita sighed, stirring sugar into her tea. "Reggie says it's OK since we love each other."

Brenda rolled her eyes. "You're not falling for that old line, are you?"

"Well. . .I do love him." Rita shot Brenda a defensive look. "He writes me poems and puts them to music. . ."

"That's nice, but not sufficient grounds to have sex with him, is it?"

Rita laughed nervously. "Of course not. Reggie says we're already a couple in God's eyes. We're committed to each other, so why wait?"

"Committed, eh? When's the wedding?"

"Now look who's being old-fashioned!"

"Explain." Although there was no unkindness in Brenda's demand, there was no way she was letting Rita get away with mindless mouthing of twentieth-century platitudes. As a sister in Christ, she owed Rita more than that.

"Well—" Rita seemed to be scrambling for words. "Reggie says we're older and more sophisticated than the people in Bible times. Did you know that in Old Testament days, girls married in their early teens? These days, folks don't get married until their twenties, or even later. Surely God doesn't expect people in love to wait for years and years!"

Brenda nodded. She'd heard the argument before, even from the lips of liberal theologians and churchmen. "Tell me, Rita, what does age have to do with doing what's right?"

"Huh?"

"Sin is sin whether you're fifteen or fifty. Truth is truth. Right?"

"Y—yes. But, Brenda, other couples in the church are doing it."

"That may be. Unfortunately, not even Christians are immune to temptation. But what has their sin got to do with you?"

A worried look crossed Rita's face. "Nothing, I guess," she said, dropping her gaze to her steaming mug.

"So each of us is responsible for our own sins, right? And Reggie won't be able to assume responsibility for you when you stand before the judgment seat of Christ, will he?"

Rita shrugged miserably and tossed her hair over her shoulder. She seemed at a loss for an answer.

"Rita, if you had a child. . .say, Angelo. . .would you send him across the street without teaching him to look for traffic first?"

"Of course not!" Rita was terribly fond of the small boy and always gave him a handful of GummiBears when he visited the pharmacy.

"Well then, why would a loving God send us into this life without giving us guidance to keep us safe?"

"I guess He. . .wouldn't."

Brenda nodded. "That's right, He wouldn't. So He's given us His laws for our own protection. Sex is one of God's greatest gifts. But it's powerful stuff and belongs within marriage. Sex outside of marriage is nothing but a lie, because it mimics a commitment that doesn't exist. And playing around with lies is as dangerous as kids playing with matches."

Rita stiffened, her hands clenching her blue mug. "I don't need to be protected from Reggie. He'd never hurt me."

"What if you turn up pregnant?"

"He'd marry me. . .right away," Rita snapped, a little too quickly.

"But, Rita—" Brenda searched the younger woman's face, "if he doesn't have the strength of character to wait now, what makes you think he'd have the strength to do the right thing and marry you? Talk is cheap."

Rita didn't bat an eye. "Of course he'd marry me. He loves me."

"But what if he demanded you get rid of the baby. . .get an abortion? How would you feel then?"

"That's not going to happen!"

Brenda didn't let up. "But what if it did?"

Rita wound a long black strand of hair around her forefinger. "I suppose I'd be broken-hearted. I don't know what I'd do. . ."

"That's just my point. God wants to protect us from that kind of pain, Rita."

Rita's jaw flexed. Something like anger flashed in her dark eyes. "Don't you understand?" she almost hissed. "I need Reggie. I can't risk losing him. He's the best thing that ever happened to me. I'd die if we broke up."

Brenda felt a wave of compassion for the dark-haired girl. "What concerns me is. . .what will happen to you if he doesn't."

In a flash of insight, she knew her assistant was already sleeping with her boyfriend. And for a moment Brenda felt an impulse to share her past as a warning to the young woman. The words bubbled to her lips, almost as if they had a life of their own. But shame, embarrassment, then finally, procrastination silenced her. She wanted to help, but the price of self-disclosure was too great. She couldn't risk it. So Brenda swallowed her confession and smiled blandly at the troubled girl across the table.

She promised herself she'd confide in Rita later, knowing full well she never would. She didn't want to open old wounds. Besides, she had her reputation as Rita's employer to consider. So, like the temple priest in the parable of the Good Samaritan, who failed to stop to help the bruised and bloody traveler on the road to Jericho, Brenda kept her mouth shut and passed by.

four

"Oh, Parnell, it's. . .lovely!" Brenda exclaimed, clapping her hands. The slap of leather against leather reverberated in the cold morning air.

"Thanks. It's turned out even better than I'd hoped. We should have two dozen senior residents moved in by Christmas."

It was clear Parnell felt great pride in his latest project, a unique housing complex for senior citizens. From where Brenda stood on the sidewalk, the cluster of twelve red-brick apartment blocks seemed to gleam in the pale wintry sunlight. Each three-story unit had four apartments per floor, with access to an elevator. Each apartment opened onto a community kitchen and common living room, thus allowing the elderly tenants a degree of social interaction not usually found in apartment living. All rooms were accessible by wheelchair. Each building also had a round-the-clock staff person to handle emergencies. There was even a chapel. Parnell had thought of everything, it seemed.

Brenda nodded and smiled at her fiancé. "Parnell the Maverick," the newspapers had begun calling him. She knew the attention made him cringe, but he put up with it. After all, the publicity was good for his project—what he referred to as "a more humane way of living for senior citizens." It thrilled Brenda that he cared enough to try to improve their lot.

"They'll be like small surrogate families. Lord knows lonely seniors need that kind of family-like environment. There can be such a thing as too much independence when you get old."

Brenda could hear the concern in his voice. She'd heard that tone before when he talked about seniors. "Parnell, why are the elderly so important to you?"

43

"Well. . .if the Lord blesses, we'll be there ourselves someday," he quipped. "But seriously, I think my grandmother is my major motivation."

"She's in a nursing home?"

"Right. She's the only grandparent I've got left, and her mind has deteriorated so much she thinks I'm my father." He looked pensive and ran his hand across his beard.

"Oh, I'm sorry. I probably shouldn't have brought it up. But in my line of work, I often see people who are dealing with elderly family members."

Parnell's face grew somber. He thrust his hands into the pockets of his gray overcoat and hunched his shoulders against the cold. "Do the families always keep visiting? Even when they're not recognized anymore?"

Brenda sensed that this was a painful and very personal issue. "No, not always. Sometimes it's just too hard on them, and they shouldn't be blamed for that."

Parnell gazed at the line the red apartment buildings cut against the pale blue sky. A faraway look crept into his eyes. "I think I loved my grandmother more than anyone. . . Granny Prudence was so kind, loving, affectionate. . .yet strong. . .like you." He glanced over at Brenda. "Do you know she prayed for my grandfather's salvation for fifty years? He converted on his death-bed."

"What a story!"

"And my father, Fergus, her only child, went into the ministry. Prudence was only a simple country woman from the Pennsylvania coal country, but she was quite proud of the fact that her son became a man of the cloth."

Brenda couldn't help smiling at this revelation. "I'll bet she's mighty proud of you, too. Have you told her about your latest project?"

"No. She probably couldn't comprehend. . .now." He lapsed into silence and turned to study the horizon once more. "But I've always talked my ideas over with her, to get her input. Fifteen years ago she told me that seniors shouldn't be stuffed into high-rise warehouses like sardines. She said she never wanted to live out her last days as a lonely old lady living in a concrete box by herself. But I guess she doesn't even remember that conversation."

The sadness in Parnell's voice tugged at Brenda's heart and she slipped her arm through his. "How long has she been sick?"

"Eight years. She went into the nursing home after she broke her hip when she was ninety-two."

"Ninety-two?"

A melancholy smile played at the corners of Parnell's mouth. "Yeah. I guess the Pierce genes are good for longevity. Her hip mended, but her mind began to go. She hasn't recognized me for three years. She doesn't even realize my father is dead."

Brenda nodded. She knew the scenario. "And when she started to call you Fergus, you couldn't bear to visit anymore?"

Parnell cleared his throat. "Well, I still went to see her, for a while. But not every month. It's a three-hour drive, so it was easy to make excuses, put it off. Each time I go, another part of me dies. Now I visit about once a year. Mostly I keep tabs on her through the nurses."

Brenda gave him a sideways hug. He felt massive and strong, like the trunk of a stately old tree. "I understand, Parnell. You did the best you could. And now you see your grandmother in each little old lady you build an apartment for."

"Yep. I guess that's about the size of it." He sighed. "It's my tribute to Prudence. She put a face on the problem of senior housing for me."

"I'm sure she'd love to know that all these folks won't be warehoused into high-rises. . .like sardines, as she put it."

Parnell gave a grunt, then a rumbling laugh that seemed to vault up from his depths—a sound of relief as if he'd just shrugged a load of timber from his shoulders. Brenda felt his mood lighten.

"I love the way the buildings are grouped around gardens," she said, nodding toward the four yet-unplanted squares of earth surrounded by red brick walkways. "The oldsters can go for walks or plant flowers or just sit on the benches and chat."

"That's the idea—to make it easier to connect with others."

"And I like the fact that you left the trees." The towering trees in the dense wooded area flanking the complex looked bare and forlorn now, but she could imagine the lush, cool greenness of their summer leaves.

"More humane living also means leaving nature intact as much as possible," Parnell went on, "not bulldozing every tree and bush in sight and covering every blade of grass with concrete. People need open spaces."

"I'm sure the seniors will appreciate their new surroundings." Brenda pulled her coat tighter against the sharp wind that whistled through the trees. She took off one of her gloves and slipped her hand into the pocket of Parnell's overcoat, entwining her fingers with his. Then she stood on her toes and planted a kiss on his cheek, just above the beard line. "I want you to know I'm proud of you, Parnell the Maverick."

He flinched, ever so slightly, as if embarrassed by the title. Then remembering how he hated being glorified, she quickly added, "But we'll keep this our little secret so you don't get a swollen head."

His face brightened, his smile setting her heart to hammering. "Thanks. No fuss or fanfare needed. I'm just using the talents God gave me." In one fluid motion he put a hand under her chin, lifted it, and leaned down and brushed her cold lips in a gesture that turned into a slow, sinking kiss.

Quivering, Brenda pulled away. Her eyes met his in a wordless exchange. "We'd better get going or we'll be late for court."

He looked for all the world like a scolded puppy. "OK. But, first, I want to tell you something important." His brown eyes darkened with intensity.

"Oh?"

"Serena's portrait," he began, referring to an oil painting of his late wife, "I removed it from the dining room."

Brenda blinked. The magnificent oil had presided over the massive walnut table, as far as she knew, for the five years of the couple's marriage. When Brenda first visited the house, the portrait was hidden under a sheet, like much of the furniture in the unused rooms. She still remembered Parnell's anger when he'd found her gazing at the likeness of the dark-haired Italian beauty. But in that anger, Brenda had seen the depth of his grief. It was, in fact, the moment she'd begun to fall in love with him. She knew that only a person who can grieve deeply can love deeply.

Now, he'd put away the portrait. That could mean only one thing.

"It was time, Brenda. Serena will always hold a special place in my heart, but you're the love of my life now."

Brenda put up her hand and pressed it against the side of his face. It felt cold from the wind. She blinked back her tears. "She told you to marry again, didn't she? When she was dying?"

"Yes, but. . .well, you don't think I'm betraying her, do you?"

Brenda framed his face between her two hands. "There's a time for everything, Parnell, and this is our time. I believe the Lord brought us together, and I also believe Serena must be pleased that you've found love again and that Angelo will have a mother. Like my grandmother said, 'The Lord gives, and the Lord takes away, and sometimes the Lord gives back again.'"

"I knew you'd understand."

"Where did you put the portrait? Not in the attic, surely?"

Parnell cleared his throat. "Well, as a matter of fact, yes. The attic seemed the logical place."

"Well, maybe, but I don't feel right about it. How would that make Angelo feel?"

Parnell's face fell. "I didn't think about that."

"How about hanging the portrait in the upstairs hallways, along with all the other family photos and portraits? That way Angelo won't feel as if I've banished his mother from the house. Anyway, I feel a connection with her; we're both mothers to the same boy, you know."

"You're a generous woman, Brenda Rafferty."

"Not really. I just think there's enough love to go around. C'mon, let's get to court before Gil Montgomery breaks bail and runs."

"We're on our way." Parnell dropped a kiss on the top of her head and steered her toward his car. "And I'll just bet his father could arrange something like that, too."

Brenda laughed uneasily as they crossed the newly dried concrete parking lot. Senator Edmund Montgomery, once investigated for taking bribes to allow laxer testing of generic drugs, had tried to buy off the prosecutor in his nephew's criminal trial two years ago. He'd almost succeeded until Parnell found out and blew the whistle. The nephew in question, Damien Montgomery, was the chief hooligan throwing the rocks that had hit Reverend Fergus Pierce's car. Brenda shivered, despite the warmth of her coat and Parnell's arm around her shoulders.

Suddenly the nerve-rattling revving of a motorcycle from the apartments across the street caught her attention. The development, Pierce Estates, was one of Parnell's low-income buildings, a rarity in the well-heeled town of Columbia. The racket was coming from a huge, black Harley being started outside Rita Andreas' apartment. Brenda recognized the rider at once.

"Reggie Lorino!"

"Who?" asked Parnell as he held the car door open for her.

"Rita's boyfriend."

"Oh, Rita—your assistant. Isn't she working today?".

Brenda nodded. "Both she and Tori are holding down the fort while I testify. But I'm afraid my worst suspicions may have just been confirmed." She glanced worriedly at Parnell as she ducked into the car. He closed the door and strode around to the driver's side, deactivating his electronic lock as he went.

"Hmm, what do you mean?" he asked as he slid into his seat and reached for the seat belt.

"It's 8:30 in the morning and Reggie's just leaving Rita's apartment. What do you think that means?" She inhaled deeply of Parnell's woodsy, masculine aftershave as he started the engine.

"Maybe he dropped in for an early breakfast?"

"Rita didn't have any breakfast," Brenda said. "That was pretty obvious when she practically fell on the packet of donuts I left for her and Tori when I left the shop thirty minutes ago. Oh, Parnell,

I'm so worried for her."

"Why? Reggie Lorino is a committed Christian musician, isn't he?"

"Well. . .supposedly." She hesitated a moment, wondering whether to say anything more.

"This can't go any further, but Rita's told me that he's been pressuring her to have sex with him."

"I see." Parnell never took his gaze from the road as he swung onto Route 29 heading toward the courthouse.

"He's using all the standard lines on her: 'Everyone's doing it.' 'It's OK because we really love each other.' 'We'll probably get married anyway. . .'"

"And she's falling for it?"

"Hook, line, and sinker."

"Why? She seems like a sensible young woman to me."

Brenda hurried on. "She is, in most cases. But when it comes to matters of the heart. . .well, I'm afraid Rita is still looking for the first man who dumped her."

"And who was that?"

"Rita never knew her father, Parnell. He abandoned her before she was even born. I think that's why she always picks the wrong men, guys who love her and leave her. I've seen it happen before. She's so hungry for love, it clouds her judgment."

Parnell shook his head sadly. "Fatherless America," he said. "It's the tragedy of our times. I tell you, Brenda, our culture really shot itself in the foot when it bought the lie that fathers are unnecessary and marriage doesn't matter. In my research for my work, I've found study after study that shows that fatherless children become troubled children and contribute to the mounting crime statistics. Did you know that the United States now leads the world in fatherless families? Over thirty percent of babies are born to single mothers. Nearly seventy percent of minority children are illegitimate. Fatherlessness is practically a national crisis."

Brenda watched the tidy suburbs pass by. Her hands tightened around her purse strap. "Yeah. I know those stats. I've done some reading on that subject myself. The two-parent family is still the best department of health, education, and welfare." Her hopes started to rise. *He understands how important fathers are. Maybe he'll have compassion for me, after all.* She felt a sudden lightness, almost a giddiness of relief, and resolved to tell Parnell the whole story over lunch, after her court appearance.

Parnell seemed thoughtful as he turned into the crowded courthouse parking lot and wound his way around, looking for an empty space. "Can you get Rita to talk to Pastor Milligan? That might help."

"I'll do that. Perhaps I could find her some reading material at the Christian book store. Rita's very dear to me, Parnell. I feel like her older sister. She doesn't have a close relationship with her mother, and her only other relative, Uncle Bob, spends his time in one mental hospital or another."

"Sad." Parnell shook his head and killed the engine. "We'll have to pray for her and put her in the Lord's hands." He reached over and stroked Brenda's hair. "But right now, I'm more concerned about you. Nervous about today?"

"A little. I've never testified in a courtroom before."

"Nothing to it. It'll be a breeze, and afterward, we'll go out for that nice lunch I promised you, OK? And I'll be in the courtroom the whole time."

"Thanks, Parnell. That helps more than you know."

Even so, Brenda couldn't shake the feeling of dread in the pit of her stomach. It went beyond concern for Rita, or anxiety over facing Gil Montgomery in the courtroom. It was a sinister, eerie kind of dread. A pit of fear in her stomach. Anticipation, waiting for something bad to happen. Almost like a premonition.

The feeling that she was about to walk into a den of lions.

five

Atop an evergreen-covered hill, the Howard County Courthouse sat like a stout, elderly gentleman shrouded in robes of sparkling pink and gray marble. A handful of buildings—old colonials restored to white-shuttered charm—stood like sentinels around the courthouse and provided premium office space for accountants, lawyers, and government officials.

The courthouse was generally a quiet, dignified place, but this morning the brick sidewalks were jammed with media personnel and curiosity-seekers. A cacophony of voices floated on the brisk air. Despite the cold, Brenda's palms began to sweat as she and Parnell walked across the parking lot. She hadn't anticipated so much media coverage. All she wanted to do was testify and leave—she absolutely did not want to appear on television!

Four white TV minivans lined the narrow road. The satellite dishes perched on their roofs looked like space machines. Brenda noticed that one enterprising crew had hooked up their lights to one of the courthouse's Dickensian light posts. Someone barked orders to a cameraman. Shutters snapped. A pack of reporters, armed with microphones, were circling the flushed-faced Senator Montgomery.

Parnell frowned. "The sharks smell blood!"

"I didn't expect coverage to be this intense," Brenda murmured.

"With a senator's son on trial? Nothing like a celebrity circus to boost ratings. Turning news into entertainment is what the media seems to do best these days. But the only one I'm concerned about is you. C'mon, let's find another entrance."

But before they could beat a retreat, a reporter spotted them. "There's Brenda Rafferty—key witness for the prosecution!"

A ripple went through the journalistic sea as all heads turned in their direction. Brenda noted that the senator used the distraction to escape, lumbering through the imposing courthouse doors with as much speed as his portly frame would allow.

"Hurry!" cried Parnell, grabbing Brenda's elbow. They broke into a run, but before they'd gone ten steps, a reporter overtook them.

"Randy O'Reilly from *The People's Voice*," announced the gnome of a man who planted himself squarely in front of Brenda, blocking her path. "As the state's main witness, Mrs. Rafferty, can you tell us if you were romantically involved with Gil Montgomery?"

Brenda gaped at the aging hippy with long, greasy gray hair and brazen questions. His gaunt face appeared almost skull-like in the wintry sunlight. Brenda saw something scurrilous in those deeply set, currant-black eyes that made her shiver. O'Reilly's reputation as Maryland's most ruthless tabloid reporter was legendary. He was a man who got the scoop, and more. Even so, the malicious tone of his question took Brenda by surprise. Desperately, she panned the crowd of reporters that now surrounded Parnell and her like hungry predators circling their prey.

With a jolt, the reality of the situation hit her: She was food for wolves.

"I. . .I—" As soon as she opened her mouth, she knew she'd made a mistake. Anything she might say to O'Reilly would sound like an admission of guilt to his readers. O'Reilly's knowing grin made her skin crawl.

Suddenly, a strong hand shot out and thrust O'Reilly backward. "Mrs. Rafferty will not dignify that question with an answer," Parnell growled. "She has better things to do. If you'll excuse us. . ."

TV cameras rolled and photographers took pictures as Parnell wrapped one arm around Brenda, pulling her as close as possible, sheltering her from the mob. With his other arm, he pushed a pathway through the crowd, jostling reporters, thundering over and over, "No comment!"

"You don't get rid of me so easily, Pierce," O'Reilly snarled as he struggled to keep up. "I'll get my answers. You're obstructing the public's right to know and..."

"Don't waste our time, O'Reilly. Libel laws protect citizens from scum peddlers like you."

Another reporter thrust a microphone in Brenda's face. "Mrs. Rafferty, doesn't this incident prove that compounding is dangerous?"

"Not at all—"

"Not when it's done correctly and the pharmacist is properly certified," Parnell broke in. "As Mrs. Rafferty is," he added as he took Brenda's hand and pulled her away from the reporters, through security at the courthouse door, and down the marble hallway. She followed meekly, glad to have him take charge.

O'Reilly and several others harassed them right to the door of Judge Henry Walling's courtroom. The gruff-looking bailiff waved away all reporters with cameras and microphones. Apparently, the judge had banned electronic media from his courtroom, Brenda surmised thankfully. O'Reilly and a few of his print media cronies, armed with notebooks and pens, took their seats at the back of the courtroom. Meanwhile, the bailiff ushered Brenda and Parnell into the witness holding area next door.

Brenda found herself in a small room with track lighting, bare except for four hard-backed chairs and a black leatherette couch. She blinked back tears as she sat down. *Oh, Lord, what's happening? I never expected to be put on trial*, she lectured herself. Then scolded, *Get a grip! Don't be such a baby!*

"OK?" asked Parnell gently, his scowl replaced with concern.

"I...think so. Just a little shaken is all."

"O'Reilly is the nastiest of the lot. I should have known he'd be here, hunting up new fodder for his gossip mill. But we'll tough it out, with God's help. Remember Proverbs 3:6 from church last Sunday?"

It took Brenda only a moment. It was one of her favorite Scriptures. " 'In all your ways acknowledge Him, and He will make straight your paths.' "

"Right," he said, squeezing her hand. "Nothing is going to happen today that God doesn't have in hand. Hang on to that promise."

❧

Parnell sat directly behind the waist-high wooden partition separating the public seating area from the courtroom proper. He watched Brenda walk to the mahogany witness box—head high, shoulders squared. The jury members followed her every move. What he wouldn't give to be able to carry this burden for her! A fierce tenderness shot through him at the sight of this woman who moved as regally as a queen in her tailored cream linen suit, blond hair swept up, neck and ears adorned with simple gold jewelry.

He battled a strong urge to take the law into his own hands, sprint across the courtroom, and wring Gil Montgomery's quarterback-sized neck with his own hands! At that moment, nothing would have given him greater pleasure than to inflict pain on the man who'd made Brenda suffer.

He locked eyes with Montgomery for a few seconds—just long enough to send a rush of adrenaline coursing through Parnell's body, preparing him to do battle for his beloved. It was an ancient, masculine response to a threat, he knew. And the threat was compounded by the fact that Montgomery—with his wild red hair tamed and trimmed, and outfitted in an expensive European suit—managed to look like a wronged celebrity as he lounged at the defense table, his high-priced lawyers buzzing around him like waiters in a fancy New York restaurant.

Parnell forced himself to look away and study his surroundings. The suffused light filtering through the long vertical blinds on the high windows lent an other-worldly feeling to the spacious, modern courtroom. The white walls, the muted tones of lavender and gray, the designer plum fabric chairs—all contributed a civility to the proceedings that, in Parnell's mind, Gil Montgomery didn't deserve. In the Old West, a man who attempted manslaughter and assault might have been lynched by now. But these days, he got to wear designer suits and to relax in a centrally-heated courtroom.

Chill out, man! Vengeance is Mine, says the Lord. Parnell knew better than to play the vigilante, but, even so, the idea was not without a certain appeal. Neither did he want Brenda to see his inner struggle. She was upset enough as it was. She didn't need to be burdened with his battles, too.

Brenda said he sometimes had a dark side to his personality. Her perception was not only unsettling, it also happened to be true, Parnell thought, grimacing. He could, at times, give in to brooding and even anger. In the gospel, Christ had called the young apostles James and John "sons of thunder" for wanting to call down fire from heaven on an unbelieving city. Much like Parnell itched to call down fire on the smug Montgomery as he tilted back his chair, arms crossed, seemingly only mildly inconvenienced by the proceedings.

Jesus had rebuked James and John, saying "You know not of what spirit you are. The Son of Man came not to destroy souls, but to save." Parnell flinched as he recalled the text. In the school of the Savior, these two hotheads became such gentle souls that toward the end of his life, John's constant refrain was "My little children. . .love one another." John the Apostle lost nothing of his ardor for justice, Parnell realized, but that ardor was transformed into a gentle mercy.

Perhaps this was the lesson he was to learn from these proceedings—to let God temper his darker instincts with mercy. But mercy came hard when he was expected to extend it to the man who had hurt his beloved. Parnell closed his eyes, shutting out Montgomery, his fancy lawyers, and his prominent father, and prayed for the grace to forgive as Christ had forgiven him.

He breathed deeply, willing the tension to drain out of his shoulders and arms. Looking down, he saw that his hands were clenched into fists. He deliberately relaxed them. Then he caught Brenda's eye and gave her a discreet thumbs-up signal. He mouthed the words, "We're in this together."

Her smile told him she'd gotten the message.

&

"Good morning, Mrs. Rafferty."

Prosecutor Melanie Bridges' voice rang out crisp and clear in the high-ceilinged courtroom. Brenda nodded to the smart, young attorney and tried to ignore Gil Montgomery's glare from the defense table. Out of the corner of her eye, she could see him sit, cross-armed, leaning back in his chair, as if he didn't have a care in the world. Her stomach was churning at the memory of his lewd behavior after their disastrous dinner date.

"Mrs. Rafferty," began Melanie Bridges in the nasal, no-nonsense tone of voice made popular by a slew of female TV anchors, "would you state, for the record, your address and occupation?"

"I am a self-employed pharmacist, licensed by the State of Maryland. My address is 12 Thunder Hill Lane."

The heavy-set female court reporter typed swiftly. Ms. Bridges paced back and forth in front of the bulldog-faced Judge Walling. She stopped in front of the witness box and glanced at the small yellow pad she was carrying.

"Mrs. Rafferty, is it your belief that Gil Montgomery switched the labels on drugs in your pharmacy?"

"Objection!" roared one of the Montgomery attorneys, a large, bald man with a nose as red as Santa Claus. Only there was no sense of kindness or good will about this man.

"Overruled." From Judge Walling's exasperated tone, Brenda guessed the previous two days of testimony had been jammed with objections. "Please continue, Mrs. Rafferty."

"Well, yes, I believe he did switch labels. Detective Lewis

found his fingerprints on the adhesive on the back. . ."

"Objection!"

"Sustained."

The unflappable Ms. Bridges raised her chin. Nothing appeared to disturb this thirty-something career woman, Brenda decided. Everything from her short, frosted hair to her tailored herring-bone suit broadcast confidence. She was young to take on the likes of the Montgomery team, but Brenda guessed Melanie Bridges possessed a will of steel behind her gold-rimmed glasses.

"Let's start at the beginning, Mrs. Rafferty—the evening you and Mr. Montgomery went to dinner at the Penthouse Suite in downtown Columbia."

Brenda took a deep breath, looked over at the jury—mostly middle-aged women—and launched into a recital of the events of that night. Gil had called for her at the pharmacy, offering to drive her home to change clothes before they left for the restaurant. She accepted his offer. She'd been tired, her emotions frazzled after receiving threatening phone calls from someone who wanted her out of Columbia, someone who seemed to deplore the fact that she was a Christian.

She recounted how Gil had helped her carry a box of supplies into her compounding office, just off the main area of the pharmacy. He'd shown great interest in her compounding equipment that evening—the ointment mixer, the high-tech scales, the canisters and bottles of drugs she used to make medicines. She'd found his interest unusual because until that night, he'd shown only contempt for her practice of compounding.

With a shudder, Brenda recalled how an emergency prescription had been phoned in by the intern at the hospital next door. She'd left Montgomery alone in her office for the length of time it took her to deliver the medication. Looking back, she didn't think he'd set up the call, but he was ready to take advantage of her absence.

"And then you returned and left for dinner?"

"Yes."

"Did you notice anything unusual or out of place in your office when you first returned from the hospital?"

"Nothing. When I came back, Mr. Montgomery was examining my ointment mixer. He even asked me how it worked."

Ms. Bridges resumed her pacing in front of the witness box. "Can you tell the court how you came to realize that the labels on the drugs had been switched by Mr. Montgomery?"

Montgomery's second attorney, a man with pock-marked skin and fatty eyelids, sprang to his feet. "Objection! Speculation! The witness did not see Mr. Montgomery switch anything."

"Sustained, Mr. Toomey," said the judge impatiently. "Please rephrase the question, Ms. Bridges."

Melanie Bridges inclined her head graciously. Without missing a beat, she continued. "Mrs. Rafferty, how did it come to your attention that certain labels had been switched?"

Brenda hesitated a moment, half expecting Attorney Toomey to object. Her gaze darted to the judge.

"You may answer the question, Mrs. Rafferty."

"The morning after the dinner date with Mr. Montgomery, I was compounding a medicinal syrup for an elderly customer, Mrs. Phillips, when I noticed the label on my jar of chromium was slightly crooked. It tilted up on the left side."

"Chromium is a drug?"

"Well, no. It's a dietary supplement used to help control blood sugar. It was one of the ingredients in Mrs. Phillips' prescription."

Ms. Bridges came to a dead stop in front of Brenda. "So you noticed the label was crooked, tipping to the left. Was that unusual?

"Yes, it was. Both my assistant and I are, shall we say, exacting. Even fastidious. We like having everything neat and orderly, right down to sticking labels on straight." Brenda glanced over at Gil Montgomery just in time to see him rolling his eyes heavenward. Brenda felt a little silly, but she wasn't going to deny the truth. Being meticulous was a necessary trait for a pharmacist, and she did like things to look neat. Even as far back as her kindergarten days, when she'd taken pains to keep her crayon colorings inside the lines.

"I see," said Ms. Bridges without expression. "What did you do then?"

"I had a very bad feeling. A hunch, you might say. So I began checking other jars for crooked labels."

"And what did you find?"

"I checked dozens of bottles and jars on the shelves. All the other labels were straight. Then I checked the drawer under my compounding counter where I keep unusually dangerous drugs. The label on the digitalis also tilted up to the left—almost as if it had been put there by a left-handed person. That in itself made me suspicious."

"Why?"

"Well, both Miss Manning and I are right-handed."

"How would that make a difference in how you put on a label?"

"Well, if a right-handed person puts on a label crookedly, the label will tilt up to the right. With a left-handed person, the label will tilt to the left."

"Objection!" Toomey roared. "Mrs. Rafferty is not a qualified expert on left-handedness."

"Overruled. Please rephrase the question, Ms. Bridges."

"Yes, your honor. Mrs. Rafferty, do you have any personal experience putting on labels crookedly?"

Brenda knew exactly the type of first-hand information the lawyer was after. "Well, yes I do, as a matter of fact. I experimented with labels to see how they would tilt if I put them on carelessly. When I used my right hand, they tilted up to the right," she said, demonstrating an upward movement of her hand. "When I used my left, the labels went to the left. Detective Lewis concurred with my findings."

"Yes, well, we'll hear from Detective Lewis later today." The young attorney checked her yellow legal pad, then resumed pacing, reminding Brenda of a prowling cheetah she'd seen in the Baltimore Zoo. "So the chromium label was deliberately placed on the digitalis bottle. Please tell the court the nature of this drug."

Brenda cleared her throat, briefly reliving the sickening shock that hit her when she realized she'd nearly dispensed digitalis instead of chromium. "Digitalis is a very dangerous drug—a heart medication derived from the foxglove plant that is deadly in amounts over tiny doses. It's a white powder that looks and feels like chromium."

Ms. Bridges nodded. "So, unless you had noticed the tilting label and stopped to investigate, you'd never have known the difference?"

"That is correct," said Brenda quietly, trying to still the tremor in her voice. "I'd never have known."

She looked past the attorneys' tables to Parnell. His eyes were trained on her. She'd been so nervous, she'd barely glanced at him since she began testifying. Now the compassion on his face encouraged her, renewing her determination. What a comfort to have him there, if not at her side, then at least across the courtroom.

"I have no further questions, your honor."

On cross-examination, Alexander Xavier Toomey seemed bent on clouding the issues with snide insinuations. "Come on now, Mrs. Rafferty," he grunted as he plodded toward the witness box. He was a squat, square man who wore his extra forty pounds like a badge of honor. "Isn't it true that you and my client had a lovers' quarrel after dinner and this charge is nothing but the fury of a woman scorned? Isn't that what this really is all about?"

Brenda gasped. Her mouth dropped open in horror. How could he. . .how dare he suggest such at thing! "Mr. Toomey, you don't seem to realize that it was I who rejected Mr. Montgomery's very inappropriate advances," she said, willing her voice to remain steady and strong in spite of the snickers from reporters at the back of the courtroom. She saw a sly wink exchanged between

Gil Montgomery and Senator Montgomery, a reddish-haired man as massive as King Henry VIII, who sat directly behind his son.

"Come, come, now, Mrs. Rafferty, we weren't born yesterday," drawled Toomey, crossing his arms over his ample belly, his brows shooting upward, making his bulging eyes appear even more bulbous. "We all know that Mr. Montgomery is the most eligible bachelor in town. Many women would give their right arm— and a lot more—to date a man of his status. Doesn't the fact that he didn't make another date with you suggest that maybe. . ."

Melanie Bridges sprang to her feet, slapping the wooden table with the palm of her hand. "Objection! Your honor, this line of questioning is harassing my client."

"Sustained."

Brenda felt like bursting into tears. She looked helplessly at Parnell. He shook his head, as if to indicate his own incredulity.

But the attacks continued in one form or another, despite Melanie Bridges' objections. Toomey was a master at the game, and he played to win.

After an hour of being grilled, Brenda wished that character assault had been his only strategy. She was exhausted keeping up with his trick questions, plays on words, sly innuendoes, and misrepresentations. He questioned everything she said in the most condescending tone, as if he'd just caught her in a lie. He tried to confuse her with numbers, weights, times, dates. He stopped just short of accusing her of making the whole story up in an effort to hide her own incompetence.

When his attack ended at last, Brenda felt emotionally and physically drained.

"I have no further questions," snapped Toomey as he spun around on his heel and marched back to the defense table with the air of a victorious general returning from war.

"Very well, you may step down, Mrs. Rafferty," said the judge.

"I have something to say, your honor," she said hesitantly. "Something important, if it please the court."

"Oh?" Walling furrowed his bushy salt-and-pepper brows.

"A little irregular, but you may proceed."

"Objection!" roared Toomey.

"Overruled, Mr. Toomey. This is my courtroom and I make the decisions here."

Brenda swallowed. Her throat felt dry and as scratchy as sandpaper. She hadn't planned to do this, but as she watched Gil Montgomery and his lawyers play their despicable games, she knew she had to publicly witness to the higher truth that guided her life. Her gaze rested on Montgomery. "I wanted to say. . . what I mean is, I want it known that I forgive Gil Montgomery for the harm he tried to inflict on me. I do not intend to seek redress in civil court."

A look of pure shock flooded Gil Montgomery's broad face. He jerked his head toward the window, refusing to respond to frantic whispers from both Toomey and the bald lawyer. A small gasp escaped a jury member.

Brenda turned to the judge. His expression revealed a measure of dignified surprise. "Ahem. . .is that all?"

"Yes, your honor."

"You may step down."

Brenda crossed the courtroom with a light step. The worst was over, she told herself. Parnell stood up, her coat over his folded arm. He handed Brenda her purse and with a grin, slid his other arm around her shoulders and shepherded her out of the courtroom.

❧

"Mrs. Rafferty! Mrs. Rafferty! Is it true that you issued a public declaration of forgiveness from the witness stand?" an eager young male reporter demanded as Brenda stepped out of the courthouse into the pale December midday sun.

"Yes. That's true."

"Could you tell us why?"

"Why did I forgive him? Because. . .Someone. . .forgave me, and I'd be pretty ungrateful if I failed to do likewise." Brenda felt for Parnell's hand. His strong fingers tightened around hers.

"Is Blackbeard here your fiancé?" the youth pressed, nodding at Parnell and thrusting his microphone closer until it was practically touching Brenda's nose.

"Hey, not so close," growled Parnell.

"Mr. Pierce and I are to be married next month."

Suddenly, the burden of the day fell away, and a joyful expectation flooded Brenda. Soon she'd be Mrs. Parnell Pierce—Parnell's wife, Angelo's mother. . .

"Mrs. Rafferty, I hate to spoil this sentimental moment," broke in a familiar reedy voice. Randy O'Reilly pushed his way to the front of the crowd of reporters, followed closely by his photographer who was clicking non-stop. "But my readers will want to know if it's true that you actually dated Gil Montgomery," he drawled, his pen at the ready.

Brenda stared at him without blinking an eye. After facing a battle tank like Alexander Toomey, she wasn't about to let this scrawny bully intimidate her. "Mr. Montgomery and I had one—and only one—dinner date. I assure you, Mr. O'Reilly, it was more like shop talk between two colleagues than a romantic rendezvous."

Parnell placed his free hand on her shoulder and squeezed protectively. "O'Reilly, I warned you—"

"I see," grunted O'Reilly. "Well, Mrs. Rafferty, if Mr. Pierce can restrain himself another moment or two, I need to ensure the public's right to know."

Brenda went still. Why did this moment feel as if it were suspended in eternity?

"On the subject of failed romances and forgiven—or unforgiven—sins, can you tell me whatever happened to that baby you bore out of wedlock as a teenager, kept for eleven months, and then abandoned?"

six

"What?" A cry something like a hoarse sob escaped Brenda's throat. Surely she couldn't have heard. . . Surely he couldn't have asked. . .

"Your daughter, Mrs. Rafferty," O'Reilly barked through a cloud of cigarette smoke while at the same time motioning his cameraman to get a close-up shot. "Emma, I believe you named her." He checked his notes, puffing on his cigarette, then flung it to the ground. "Born in Portage County, Ohio. She'd be about twelve years old now, wouldn't she? Can you tell us why you abandoned her?"

"I. . .I don't. . ." The pitiful words stuck in Brenda's throat. She didn't dare look at Parnell. Couldn't. Couldn't bear to see his face as her world shattered, crushed beneath O'Reilly's heel like the cigarette he was grinding out on the pavement. Then fierce maternal love took over. "I never abandoned Emma. I'd never do such a thing, you—you mudraker! I had to give her up for adoption."

"Had to give her up, eh?"

"How dare you call it abandonment!" Brenda's anger surged like electricity, energizing her.

"What else would you call giving a child away after eleven months?" O'Reilly didn't sound in the least perturbed. He grinned, baring his large, nicotine-stained teeth.

Brenda clenched her fists, tight, digging her nails into her palms. She wanted to slap him. Instead, she bit down on her lower lip and prayed silently. *Lord, give me self-control. Don't let me stoop to his level.* "Mr. O'Reilly, as any woman who's given up a child to adoption will tell you, that decision is the most difficult one she'll ever have to make; however, it was also my most

responsible act. I gave Emma up because it was best for her."
Brenda swallowed hard against the tears that threatened. *Not now! Don't let them see you cry!*

"And why was it best—as you put it—for your daughter?"

She hesitated only a moment. "Because I was too young and immature at that time to bring up a child properly. Also, after eleven months of trying to be a single parent, I realized that a child does better with both a mother and a father." The edge left her voice; her anger drained away, leaving her sad and painfully empty inside.

"How quaint, old-fashioned, and chock full of family values," muttered O'Reilly. He snorted and bared his teeth again.

Brenda looked away. *Emma. Emma. It's been so long since I've heard your name.* For a moment, she forgot about O'Reilly, Parnell, and the crowd of hungry reporters. She barely noticed the cameras clicking and flashing furiously. Brenda closed her eyes tight, transported to another time, another place. Suddenly, as if in a dream, she felt a familiar hand on her shoulder. Her eyes shot open.

"This interview is over," Parnell thundered. With his other hand he grabbed O'Reilly's collar. "Over! Do you understand? Leave her alone, scumbag! How low will you vermin stoop for a story?"

Randy O'Reilly cackled as he tried to break free of Parnell's grasp. "Hey, man, this is no figment of my imagination, even if it is news to you. They don't call me Randy the Scoop King for nothing. Really, Pierce, you don't expect me to pass up this juicy little tidbit, do you? Why, I think I've even scooped you! Didn't the little lady tell you?"

The malice in O'Reilly's tone struck Brenda like a slap on the face. She scrambled for a metaphor to understand him. *He's a predator,* she decided. *A wolf, a wild dog, some beast that feeds off human flesh.*

"Go back to the pit you crawled out of," Parnell said, his voice ominously low and brittle.

"OK with me." O'Reilly pocketed his notebook with a smirk.

"I got what I came for."

The cameras continued their assault as Brenda chanced a side-long glance at Parnell. His lips had thinned into a taut line, as if chiseled from granite, though a muscle jerked in his jaw. He'd let go of O'Reilly and stood staring straight ahead, arms at his sides, eyes narrowed and dark. *He's angry at me*, Brenda thought. She shuddered. Shock pounded through her body like waves ravaging the seashore. Her heart raced; the palms of her hands felt damp.

She stood immobilized until Parnell suddenly grabbed her arm and pulled her through the crowd of reporters and gawkers. Moving like a sleepwalker, she followed him across the black-topped parking lot, hearing the questions hurled by reporters but finding herself unable to formulate any answers.

"Mrs. Rafferty, is it true you nearly killed one of your customers?"

"Mrs. Rafferty, what will you do if Gil Montgomery is acquitted?"

"Mrs. Rafferty, have you ever heard from your daughter?"

"Mrs. Rafferty, Mrs. Rafferty. . ."

Everything swirled around her in slow motion, as if she were in some underwater scene. A strange sensation of disconnection engulfed her. She seemed to be watching herself from outside her body as she climbed into the passenger seat of Parnell's car. She watched him fasten the seat belt around her, jerk the gear stick into place, and tear out of the parking lot.

As the bare trees and suburban split-level houses streaked by, Brenda dug her nails into the flesh of her palms. Emma. The missing piece of her life. Even now, all these years later, the shock of hearing her baby's name brought back the old, searing pain. The pale green walls of the adoption agency. The social worker. Laying her sleeping daughter, barely a toddler, in the woman's arms. The agony of walking away without a backward look lest she be tempted to grab her child and run and run. . .and never stop running.

Dully, she wondered why Parnell had turned into the parking lot of an unfamiliar apartment complex. *He doesn't own these buildings.* Another thought tugged at the edge of her consciousness, something bothersome that wouldn't let go.

Suddenly, she remembered. She hadn't told Parnell the news. He'd had to hear it from someone else. Why hadn't she listened to her mother and told him sooner? But he knew now. . .about the baby she'd conceived, borne, struggled to support by herself and finally had to give up for adoption. The missing sliver of her heart. The secret she'd hidden, like a coward. Yes, he knew the truth now—the whole, sickening truth.

Parnell snapped off the engine and turned to face her. She caught her breath. He was deathly pale, but his eyes were hard, black, unforgiving. Their dark sheen frightened her. Tears pricked her eyelids, and she looked away quickly.

"Why didn't you tell me?" he said through clenched teeth. "How could you have kept this to yourself? I thought you loved me."

Cold fear spread outward from her stomach, chilling her entire body. She sat, mute.

Parnell raked his hand through his black hair with a savage thrust. "Why, Brenda? Why? We're about to be married!"

"Oh, God! What have I done?" What she'd intended to be a silent prayer tumbled out and hung heavily in the air between them. Parnell said nothing for a long time. Dread made her heart pound so hard she wondered if he could hear it. She'd never seen him this angry.

"Did it slip your mind?" he asked dryly.

Brenda flinched and looked down at her hands, twisting and untwisting them in her lap. Her eyes narrowed, lost focus. "I'm sorry," she said quietly. "I didn't mean to hurt you. I was going to tell you. . ."

"When? On our wedding day? At the altar, maybe?" He let out a raspy laugh.

Brenda took a deep breath and struggled to keep back her tears.

Oh, God, please help him understand. . . Biting her lip, she looked up.

"Well? Answer me!"

His anger felt like a hard fist in her belly. Mere words could not possibly undo the damage that had been done. On the other hand, she had to try. She had the sinking feeling her faith was about to be tested.

She cleared her throat and looked him squarely in the eye, refusing to let his anger intimidate her. "I'll try to explain as best I can," she began. "When I was a senior in high school, I went through a rebellious stage. I was out of control, caught up in the spirit of the times. As a little girl, I'd been close to Jesus, but somehow, faith slipped away when I hit my teens. Being hip and cool became the most important thing.

"Of course, I fell in with the wrong crowd, including a guy who fed me the same lines Reggie Lorino is feeding Rita. Brad swore up and down he loved me. He insisted we had the right to express our . . .'love.' What did our parents know with their outdated morals? It was mature and liberating to act on our feelings. All the popular songs said so. After a while, he wore me down. . . No, that's not quite true. I let myself be worn down. What I did, I did to myself. No one forced me to."

She watched Parnell's profile apprehensively. What was he thinking? She couldn't tell. He stared straight ahead, rigid as rock. Gathering her courage, she plunged on. "Brad and I had. . .a relationship. . .for about six months. We felt so smug and pleased with ourselves. Then I learned I was pregnant."

She fell silent, a hardness choking her throat. Furiously, she swallowed against the lump of emotion. She wouldn't cry. Not now. She'd proven herself weak enough already. Perhaps Parnell despised her. Perhaps he couldn't even stomach her presence. She felt like a lone swimmer far out at sea. Loneliness surrounded her like a mist, threatened to drag her down to the bottom of the ocean, to drown her.

"Go on," he said, still not looking at her.

"I was so ashamed. . .I couldn't tell my parents. I didn't even tell Brad, not at first. Instead, I talked him into running away together. Eloping, I called it. That sounded more romantic. After all, we were in love, I reasoned. Lots of people were living together. Brad liked the idea. He was only too glad to escape from his strict family and high school."

Brenda paused, hoping Parnell would say something. When he didn't, she hurried on, as if trying to outrun old ghosts. "We went to Ohio because he had a friend there who played in a rock band. Brad worked at a gas station and I got a job at a convenience store. We were two kids playing house."

Parnell hung his head, folding one arm and putting the thumb and index finger of the other hand on the bridge of his nose. "And your parents? Didn't they try to stop you?"

"Oh, they tried. But I was eighteen. I told them to hang loose, that Brad and I would get married eventually. I really believed that. . .until I told Brad about the baby. He went ballistic. Smashed his fist into the wall, stomped up and down the apartment, swearing and kicking furniture. Said he was too young to be tied down. Told me to get rid of it, to have an abortion. When I refused, he ran off. I heard from his rock group friend that he'd hitchhiked to California and joined a Moonie cult."

"So. . .you were alone in Ohio?"

"Yes. I kept my job and my baby. But I never told my family I'd given birth, nor did I come home to visit. I'd messed up my life too badly. I was too proud." She ducked her head, suppressing a little smile. "My mother still calls me her stubborn one. I wasn't going to ask for help, if it killed me. And it nearly did."

Parnell looked at her then, eyes wide with astonishment. "You mean to tell me you had a baby and never told your parents?"

Brenda sighed. "Crazy, huh? But there was a reason for my madness. I was too proud to crawl back to my family, begging for help. If I could make it by myself with my baby—move up in my job, get a raise, get myself established—then I was going to tell them about Emma. My plan was to tell my family only when

I didn't need help anymore."

Parnell groaned. "Why? Didn't you think they'd help you?"

"Of course I knew they'd help. That wasn't the point. The point is I didn't want to accept their help. If I could make it by myself, I wouldn't have to admit I'd made a mistake. I wouldn't have to ask God and my family for forgiveness. I could continue to thumb my nose at their values. I could say, 'See, I broke all the rules, and nothing bad happened. Who needs God?' Like I said, Parnell, I was stubborn."

"I can see that." Parnell focused his gaze on the red brick apartment building in front of them. Several young boys tumbled out of the front door and began to play tag on the sidewalk.

He can't stand to look at me, she thought. *Who can blame him?*

"After my two weeks of maternity leave, I put Emma in the cheapest day care center I could find," she continued. "When she started to get sick—those centers are like germ factories—I missed too much work and lost my job. Then I lost my car. Sometimes I had to choose between food and paying the rent. I wouldn't go on welfare. When I found another job—typing in an insurance office—I had to get up at 4 A.M., dress Emma, take two busses across town, and leave her in day care for fourteen hours."

Parnell shook his head, but said nothing.

"After six months of this, my health began to go. I started blacking out. The center didn't give good care. Emma hurt herself several times, falling off chairs and down stairs. One time, an older child almost broke her foot, hitting her with a piece of pipe the plumbers had left lying around in the bathroom. . ." Brenda shuddered as she flashed back to the horror of that telephone call at work. She could still hear her nine-month-old baby screaming in the background. "I had to take her on the bus to the hospital because I couldn't afford a taxi or an ambulance. . ."

Brenda broke off, turning to gaze out the car window. On the sidewalk in front of the apartment building, the group of boys were now playing a game of marbles. She guessed they were second- or third-graders. How much of her daughter's life she'd missed!

"All this time, I'd stayed away from church," she said at last. "But at the hospital that day, I went to the chaplain. I broke down in his office. He urged me to think about what was best for Emma, to consider adoption. I told him that was the cruelest thing I'd ever heard, but, in my heart, I was afraid he might be right.

"Emma deserved a better life. It wasn't her fault I'd made some really foolish choices. The poor little thing almost never saw me. She needed a mom to love her all day, not a succession of child-care workers. I felt like the mother in the Bible story about King Solomon. Two women claimed a baby, so the king ordered it cut in two. The real mother gave up the child rather than see it hurt."

Something flickered over Parnell's face before he checked it. "So you gave her up?"

Brenda hesitated. "Not right away," she said. "I hung on several more weeks, until we both ended up in the emergency room. I blacked out when I was stepping off the bus, Emma in my arms. She hit her head on the curb and ended up with a concussion. I broke my arm. Then the doctors discovered I had mononucleosis."

She heard Parnell stifle a groan. "And then?"

"The doctor told me the stress was killing me, that I couldn't go on like that. Before I could stop them, they contacted my parents. The first time Louise and Don saw their granddaughter, she was bandaged up, in a hospital crib." Brenda's eyes filled with tears.

"What did they say?"

"Oh, they were willing to help me, of course."

"But you didn't let them?"

"I considered it. But Emma deserved more, a proper family with a father and a home. I did my homework, Parnell. This wasn't a snap decision. I studied the statistics, read the books. Kids, especially girls, do better with two parents. I loved, and still love, my daughter. But no way was I going to hurt her any more than I already had."

Parnell grunted. Brenda wondered what he was thinking.

"It was my judgment call, Parnell. Mom and Dad helped me examine all sides of the issue, but in the end, it came down to my decision. And, God help me, I made the best one I could. I was a sick, worn-out kid myself. There was nothing ahead for Emma but years and years of day care centers while I tried to provide for her. What kind of life would that have been? What did I have to offer her?"

"A mother's love," he said, his words driving a sword through her heart.

"Yes," she whispered. "But it was also my love that caused me to give her to a mature, loving couple who could provide a real Christian home. Sometimes love by itself isn't enough. It takes two people to make a baby, Parnell. And it takes two to bring up a child."

"So you just. . .gave her away."

"Yes. It was the hardest thing I've ever done, but I still believe it was the best thing for Emma. I couldn't let my mistake blight her life. . .please, try to understand. I didn't abandon her."

"Uh huh," was all he said.

"In a strange way, Emma gave me the gift of life," Brenda continued, thinking out loud. "When I saw how much I'd hurt everyone I loved, especially my own child, I finally came to realize what sin is all about. Only then did I know, really know in my heart, how much I needed a Savior. In my smug pride, I thought I could handle my own life. Emma taught me I couldn't."

"Sin? You saw your daughter as sin?"

"No! No! The sin was mine, not hers. Emma was an innocent, sacred little life made in the image of God."

"That you gave away." His voice had a bitter ring.

"Yes." Brenda swallowed hard. He seemed to be demanding that she say the hard words. Well, she'd give him what he wanted. Bracing herself, she turned to face him. "Yes, Parnell, I gave her away. I was an immature young girl, and I didn't think I could bring her up alone."

The words seemed to echo around the spacious interior of the car, bouncing back in recrimination. Yes, she was guilty of giving her daughter away. Her own flesh and blood. Old guilt flooded back in a tidal wave, and she fought desperately to keep back the tears that would surely undo her.

"I'm sorry, Brenda, but I need time alone," Parnell said flatly as he turned the ignition key. A scarcely perceptible tremor crossed his face as he threw the car into gear.

Brenda nodded, too choked up to trust herself to say anything. He seemed totally preoccupied with his own thoughts, almost unaware of her presence. If he did notice her quiet crying, he made no move to comfort her. Instead, he drove silently through the labyrinth of streets until he pulled up in front of her house.

He didn't turn off the engine and he didn't look at her. Clutching her purse, Brenda opened her own door and stepped out.

He drove away without a word.

❧

Moving in slow motion, Brenda took her key from her purse and let herself into her house. The roar of Parnell's car subsided into an unnerving silence. She drew the door closed and leaned back against it, making no move to take off her coat.

Streams of thin, watery sunlight filled the living room. The room, usually cheerful, now seemed to mock her with brittle emptiness. The cold sheen of the yellow and green chintz couch, the glare of the glass-topped round coffee table covered with glass figurines that looked like chips of ice. Suddenly everything seemed hard, frozen, without soul.

After many minutes, her mental numbness began to thaw. But as it did, the pain came into sharp focus, like an anesthetic wearing off after an operation. She sagged against the door, feeling as if she would never again have the energy to move. She felt only half alive. She slid her hands, palms down, against the soft wool of her coat, hoping the sense of touch would anchor her to the real world. "I've lost them all," she murmured to herself. "Emma, Parnell, even Angelo. . ."

She'd forgotten to put on her gloves, she noticed absently. Had she left them in the courthouse? In Parnell's car? Dropped them on the street? They were made of fine red leather, a Christmas gift from her mother last year.

Mother! I'll call Mother! She'll know what to do!

That hope propelled her into action. She jerked away from the door, throwing her purse and sending her keys clattering across the hardwood floor, grabbed the telephone receiver, and punched in her mother's office number. Her hand tightened around the receiver. Every ring seemed an eternity. Finally, after four rings, the someone on the other end picked up.

"Mom! I've got to talk. . ."

"Hello," came a soft, cultured voice on the answering machine. Her mother's professional tone. "You've reached the counseling office of Dr. Louise Ford. . ."

"Oh, no!"

"I'm with a client at the moment or on the other line, so please leave your name and number. Or if you prefer, you may begin transmitting a fax now."

Brenda slammed down the phone, almost toppling the unit off the end table. She sank down to the floor, still bundled in her long wool coat. She hugged her knees to her chest, her golden hair falling over her bent legs. *This has all been a nightmare. It's too horrible to be real.*

She sat huddled on the floor, rocking back and forth, moaning from time to time. Bleakly, she remembered that she'd forgotten to turn up the central heat that morning. The damp cold seeped into her body, licking her very bones. *I've lost him. I know I have. Who can I call? I need to talk to someone.*

Suddenly, she drew herself up. She knew who she had to talk to, wondering in dazed amazement why she hadn't thought of Him before.

seven

"Lord, how could You let this happen to me?" Brenda cried aloud, her eyes blurring as she stared at the steely square of sky visible through her large, living-room window. She drew in a ragged breath. "How could You, Lord? My life's just been trashed! Don't You care?"

She buried her face in her hands, giving vent to her grief. *Oh, Lord, why did You let this wound be ripped open again? Wasn't it enough that I gave Your child the gift of life? Or that I went through torture to give her a better life? What more do You want from me?*

No answer came. She wept until her tears were spent, using the heels of her hands to wipe her wet cheeks. Then she fished a tissue out of her pocket and blew her nose. For what seemed like an eternity, she sat watching dully as the sky darkened. A fierce December wind wailed around her small Cape Cod, battering the loose storm windows. The old wooden frames rattled under the assault.

Parnell had promised to replace the storm windows, she recalled. She doubted that job would get done, not now. In fact, she didn't think Parnell would be around much anymore. After the public humiliation he'd suffered because of her, how could she blame him if he never wanted to see her again?

Parnell wasn't exactly a cuckolded husband, but he was a deceived fiancé. Even if the deception had been by omission. If Randy O'Reilly had his way, Parnell would be the laughingstock of the town by the evening news. What an opportunity for O'Reilly to boost his rating—a sordid story about the chief witness at a highly publicized trial, plus pulling one over on a wealthy land developer. And she'd handed O'Reilly that opportunity on a silver platter!

Brenda shivered, hugging her knees tighter to her chest. The house felt cold, damp, tomblike. Like her spirits. "Oh, Lord, where is Your will in all this. . .mess?" she cried. "It was bad enough having O'Reilly ambush me. . .but what about Parnell? Why couldn't he have understood about Emma? Like Mom said he would? Maybe if he'd learned some other, less public, way. . ."

If only. . . If only. . . If only I'd told him myself. . .

Brenda clenched her eyes shut against the new flood of tears. *But would that really have made any difference? Really? Parnell doesn't seem to understand about adoption. He must think I'm a monster for giving up an eleven-month-old child. Why else would he take off without saying a word? I was afraid this would happen. That's why I put off telling him. . .*

She was about to give in to a deluge of self-pity when something nudged her conscience—a still, small voice that seemed to whisper, *So, it's all Parnell's fault?* Brenda caught her breath, then inhaled sharply. Suddenly she had the distinct feeling that she wasn't being entirely honest with herself or with God. She tried to resist that conviction, to defend herself, to deny her responsibility. But after several moments of wrestling with herself, she surrendered. Brenda had been a Christian long enough to recognize the beating of the Holy Spirit's wings against her heart's door.

OK, Lord, I admit it. I let my stupid pride stop me from telling him. I was so concerned with what he'd think of me, so afraid he'd discover I wasn't Miss Perfect Christian after all. I'm so sorry, Lord. Please forgive me. . .not only for my pride, but for my lack of courage. I failed You, Lord, through my silence. And now. . .now I've ruined everything. . .

Brenda sobbed, leaning her head on her coat, which covered her bent knees. Her golden hair tumbled over the black fabric. The wool scratched her wet face. She hugged her legs tighter, weeping and letting the pain seep out like infection from a lanced sore. "Lord, this hurts too much! I know it's my fault for not telling him. I accept that. . .but it doesn't make it hurt less!"

The drumming of the rain grew louder as it lashed against the aluminum siding. Brenda opened her eyes and watched the last of the light trailing through the window, scattering across the floor. Sheets of water sluiced down the large glass panes. Thunder rumbled—like a voice from heaven.

"Oh, Lord, you desire truth in the inward parts," she prayed. "I admit my weaknesses and sins, Lord. Cleanse me from secret faults. No matter how badly I feel, help me to believe Your promise to bring good out of every situation for those who love You. Lord, I trust You—at least most of the time. Help me to trust You always."

                              ❧

Brenda didn't know how much time had passed. The persistent knocking on her front door roused her from a light sleep. Her legs were stiff. Her feet tingled with pins and needles as she jumped up and bounded over to the door, hoping against hope it was Parnell.

Louise Ford stood outside, one hand clutching a yellow scarf around her hair, the other fending off the rain with a ruby red umbrella. "Brenda! I just saw you and Parnell on the evening news!" she exclaimed at she stepped inside the house. "I called the pharmacy. Rita said you never came back, so I figured you were here. . ."

"The news? Oh, no!"

Her mother took off her wet blue raincoat and hung it on the clothes tree. "Oh, dear, you didn't see it? Dreadful. Absolutely dreadful. I don't know why these reporters insist on mud-raking at every opportunity. . ." She broke off, rubbed her arms, and looked around. "Darling, is your heat pump broken? It's freezing in here and you've still got your coat on."

"Oh, I forgot. . . It's been a trying day, to say the least." Brenda hurried over to the wall thermostat and flipped the switch. Immediately, the pump kicked in with a familiar rumble. She started to unbutton her own coat.

"Have you eaten?" her mother asked, eyeing her closely.

Brenda couldn't help smiling. "Once a mother, always a mother. As a matter of fact, no. I haven't eaten since breakfast. I was so nervous about the Montgomery trial, all I could gag down was a piece of toast. Parnell was going to take me to lunch, but then. . ." Suddenly she found her throat closing over and she couldn't speak.

Louise Ford didn't need to hear more. She marched over to the kitchen next to the L-shaped living room, tied Brenda's pink apron around her jade silk shirtdress, and began rooting in the refrigerator. "You've got eggs, mushrooms, and tomatoes, Brenda," she called. "How about an omelette, some toast, and a nice cup of hot, sweet tea?"

"Sounds lovely. You do the eggs. I'll make the tea."

Somehow the normalcy of making a meal with her mother helped Brenda ease back into the familiar flow of life, putting a little distance between her and the shock of the day's happenings. The end of the world hadn't come that afternoon when Parnell drove away in angry silence; it only felt that way.

Now there were eggs to eat and reality to deal with. Brenda closed her eyes and breathed a prayer of thanksgiving for God's continual care before cutting into the fluffy omelette. "Mmm. You still make the best eggs, Mom," she said between mouthfuls.

Across the rose-colored kitchen table, Louise Ford sat nibbling on a piece of dry toast and sipping a cup of black tea. She waited until her younger daughter had eaten her fill before talking.

"More tea, dear?"

"Just half a cup, Mom. Thanks. That was delicious. I feel revived."

"I shouldn't wonder. You looked like death warmed over when I came in. Now that I've seen the TV version of what happened, I'd like to hear the real story—from you."

Brenda sighed and sat back in the cushioned metallic swivel chair, crossing her arms. "I guess you could say Randy O'Reilly ambushed me. After I testified, as I was coming out of the courthouse, he rushed up out of nowhere and asked what had happened to the baby I gave up for adoption. Accused me of abandoning her. . ."

Her mom reached across the table and touched Brenda's forearm. "Darling, that must have been a dreadful shock."

"Oh, Mom! I couldn't believe it. Part of me still can't believe it. Why would O'Reilly do such a. . .mean-spirited thing? What purpose does it serve? Emma has nothing to do with Gil Montgomery's trial."

Mrs. Ford shook her head. "To get the scoop, my dear. Especially one that panders to scandal and prurient interests."

Brenda frowned into her teacup. "Well, O'Reilly certainly got the scoop on me, didn't he? And right in front of Parnell. But do you know the worst part, Mom? The worst part is that it's all my fault. If I'd told Parnell like you suggested, O'Reilly couldn't have taken him by surprise like that."

Mrs. Ford patted Brenda's arm. "I know, I know, dear. I'm sure you feel dreadful about that. But don't be too hard on yourself. It was just a case of unfortunate timing. . ."

"No, Mom," Brenda cut in. "Bad timing, yes. But it was more than that. It was also my pride. I didn't want Parnell to think badly of me, so I kept putting off telling him. . .and now. . .now he's so mad, he tore out of here without looking back. He didn't say a word during the whole drive home."

Compassion shone in Mrs. Ford's china blue eyes. "He's angry, shocked, hurt, I shouldn't wonder. Remember, Parnell has always been a man of deep, passionate emotions. And he does have a tendency to brood. Give him some time

Brenda pushed away from the table. "Well, what else can I do? He said he needed time. In fact, that's all he said."

"Well, there you have it, darling. We'd all need time to assimilate such a shock."

Brenda added some milk to her already tepid tea and stirred miserably. "Oh, Mom, I thought Emma was a closed chapter in my life. Now O'Reilly throws it in my face like. . .something sordid. I made a mistake, I know. . ."

"For which our Lord forgave you," her mother broke in. "He

wiped the slate clean. And you honored Him by respecting His gift of life. Now you need to respect yourself for what you did. God honors you for doing the right thing, even if the world doesn't."

Brenda smiled at her mother. Her carefully coiffed hair, so like a halo, made her resemble an angel—a mature, maternal-looking angel. "Thank you, Mom. I needed to hear that. But the way Parnell reacted, you'd think I'd committed a crime."

Mrs. Ford sipped her tea thoughtfully. "Maybe he knows a situation where adoption didn't work out well. That's one possibility. Or maybe he doesn't know much about adoption at all, and he's reacting out of ignorance, even fear. Or maybe he's just hurt and angry because you didn't confide in him in the first place."

Brenda fell silent, traveling back a dozen years in her memory. Finally, she blurted, "Mom, I made the right decision about Emma all those years ago, didn't I?"

"I believe you did, darling."

Brenda shook her head. "Oh, Mom, I was so self-centered, so into rejecting everything you and Dad stood for. But even if I'd been more mature, I'm still convinced kids do better with two parents."

A look of worry flitted across Louise Ford's even features. "I still wish you'd told us you needed help."

"So do I, Mom. So do I. But, as you said yourself, I was always your stubborn one. I felt so ashamed, not only of getting pregnant, but of shacking up with Brad. . .and then, the humiliation of his dumping me. I used to think that I wasn't even good enough for him! I figured that I'd made my own bed, and I had to lie in it."

Brenda's mom looked at her intently. "Don't forget we committed Emma into the Lord's care, just like the mother of Moses did when she placed him in the bulrushes. The social worker assured us she placed Emma with a committed Christian family."

"You're right, Mom. Emma is in the Lord's hands."

"So hold up your head, my girl, and move on. Looking back only brings more pain."

"I only wish Parnell would see it that way. I can't shake the feeling that he believes I'm a terrible person because I gave up my daughter." Brenda glanced over at the white phone hanging next to the stove. She often took Parnell's calls there while she was cooking a meal or washing dishes. "You know, Mom, Parnell puzzles me a little."

"In what way?"

"His stand on life issues, specifically abortion."

"Oh?"

"Well, you know how committed he is to the elderly," began Brenda, putting her thoughts together as she talked. "He can see the dignity of life on that end of the spectrum, but he doesn't seem to completely appreciate the dignity of life before birth. The other day he said he could see situations when abortion might be the best alternative, or the lesser of two evils."

"The so-called hard cases, right?"

"Yeah. Says he's pro-choice."

Mrs. Ford rested her chin on top of her folded hands. Her red nails glistened in the light from the Tiffany lamp over the table. "Parnell is a compassionate man," she said. "Anyone can see that in his love for his son and his work with the elderly and the poor. But in the area of abortion, his compassion seems to be misguided. Perhaps he hasn't studied the issues and thought things through."

Brenda shrugged. "He says it's a woman's decision."

Mrs. Ford smiled sardonically. "That can be a convenient cop-out, even for a compassionate man. It excuses men from having to wrestle with the subject. We know that abortion does no favor for women, or teenage girls." She narrowed her eyes. "Can you imagine trying to live with yourself now if you'd had an abortion?"

Brenda shook her head. "No. I'm so thankful I didn't fall for that option, at least. Brad tried to bully me into it, you know."

"Well, that was the easy way out for him, wasn't it? Since you wouldn't abort, he took the second easiest way out and ran away. These days, I'm seeing more and more women in my counseling practice who are still recovering from an abortion they had five, ten, even fifteen years ago. There's even a name for it, Post Abortion Syndrome. It's a delayed grieving reaction."

Silence fell between the two women. Outside, the rain beat steadily against the house. Inky blackness lapped at the kitchen window. Feeling suddenly vulnerable, Brenda sprang up from the table and crossed the kitchen to close the curtains.

Mrs. Ford began clearing away the dishes. "We need to pray for Parnell, Brenda. Pray that the Holy Spirit will open his heart to the truth that all of life is a precious, seamless garment. We can't honor and protect it on one end and not the other."

Brenda yanked the navy and pink flowered curtains across the window over the sink. She turned and leaned against the stove, surveying her mother. "The seamless garment? That sounds familiar."

"It comes from the Bible. When the soldiers crucified the Lord, they cast lots for His garment rather than tearing it and ruining it. Christ's cloak was woven all in one piece, like the gift of life from beginning to end is all the same piece of God's handiwork."

"That's a powerful image, Mom."

"Have you thought about why God let this incident outside the courtroom happen just when it did?" Louise Ford asked as she carried the plates to the sink.

Brenda started. Her mouth suddenly felt dry. She had the distinct feeling her mother was going to say something important, very important. "What do you mean?"

The dishes clattered against the stainless steel sink. "O'Reilly's little stunt today might force Parnell to face the questions of abortion and adoption head on." Mrs. Ford scraped Brenda's plate and began to load the dishwasher. "Because of you, these issues have suddenly become personalized for him. Now he has to search his conscience and take a stand, especially on abortion. He can't keep on evading forever."

It made sense. Brenda nodded silently, chewing her bottom lip.

"We don't always choose our battles, dear. Sometimes we wake up in the middle of a battlefield where we'd rather not be fighting. But God puts us exactly where He wants us—in a particular time, place, and century, for that matter. As Christians living in the century of genocide, euthanasia, and abortion, I believe we're called to witness to the gospel of life."

Brenda shivered and wrapped her arms around herself. "I'd never thought of it that way. We do live in a culture of death, where convenience is king, don't we?" Her hands clenched, and she looked imploringly at her mother. "Oh, Mom! Why did I take the easy way out by keeping the truth from Parnell? Why didn't I tell him?"

eight

"Oh, mercy!" Rita Andreas's voice rang shrilly across the pharmacy. "Brenda! Have you seen today's paper yet?"

A chill of apprehension passed through Brenda. She'd purposely avoided all newspapers, radio, and TV since O'Reilly's attack yesterday. "No," she called back, never lifting her gaze from the paperwork on her desk. Suddenly, she found it impossible to concentrate on the complicated Health Maintenance Organization stipulations she'd been studying. She put the booklet down.

Rita careened around the corner, her white pharmacy coat open, long black hair flying. "Randy O'Reilly's 'Scoop of the Day' column!" she cried, brandishing a folded-up newspaper. "It's awful!"

Brenda looked up from her desk and took the paper from Rita. *No point in putting off the inevitable any longer. Lord, help me.*

Steeling herself, she unfolded the paper.

It was worse, much worse than she'd expected. The huge, half-page photograph of Parnell and herself grabbed her attention first. In the picture, she looked dazed, her gaze downcast, while Parnell . . .the photographer had captured the look on his face at the exact moment the truth had dawned on him. The suspicion in his narrowed eyes had just been replaced by bleak dismay. His mouth was twisted in the pained expression of betrayal. His face looked as desolate as wasteland in Alaska.

Brenda shuddered. *He'll never be able to forgive me for this!*

Under the stark black and white photograph, the headline screamed: "Montgomery Trial Witness Has Dirty Little Secret—Get Rid of The Kid!"

Brenda's heart lurched. She didn't want to read any further. But for Parnell's sake, she forced herself. "Brenda Rafferty, owner of Rafferty Pharmacy and proponent of the controversial new practice of medicinal compounding, admits to a dating relationship with the accused, although she's quick to insist the dates were platonic. Gil Montgomery suggests otherwise. Perhaps the lady doth protest too much. Come, come, Mrs. Rafferty, do you think we were born yesterday?

"But in what turned out to be the biggest, most amusing 'Scoop of the Day,' her current fiancé, land baron Parnell Pierce, learned (much to his bourgeois surprise) that his intended was already a mother. Seems Mrs. Rafferty forgot to tell the wealthy gent about that illegitimate kid she put up for adoption after a teenage fling. Some might not put it so kindly. After all, getting rid of an eleven-month-old kid sounds like abandonment to this writer. Well, never mind, Mrs. R., it's a free country; we all make mistakes. . .but not all of us hide them under the cloak of evangelical Christianity. . ."

And so it went. On and on. O'Reilly even included several salacious comments from Gil Montgomery about their "deep and affectionate relationship." Brenda nearly gagged as she remembered how he'd tried to physically force himself on her, and wondered what kind of relationship existed between Montgomery and O'Reilly. Had the reporter been paid to make the wealthy senator's son look good? Or did O'Reilly just relish writing hate-filled columns, wringing as much scandal out of each detail as possible? She could almost hear his cackle now.

Suddenly, Rita's worried face dipped into her line of vision. "Brenda! Is this true?"

Brenda blinked and drew a deep, shuddering breath. "Yes, Rita. It's true. I had a baby out of wedlock. When the father deserted me, I was too proud and ashamed to ask my parents for help. I tried to raise her alone. . .but, in the end, I put her up for adoption. I didn't forget to tell Parnell. I just kept putting it off because I didn't want him to find out how weak I was, didn't want to hurt him. But I ended up hurting him even more."

Rita's mouth dropped open. After a moment she said quietly, "Brenda, I'm so sorry, so sorry. It must have been terrible for you." Her eyes misted over.

Brenda laughed bitterly. "Perhaps militant atheist O'Reilly

wasn't far off the mark accusing me of hypocrisy and hiding behind my religion."

A customer rang the service bell on the counter, but neither woman moved. Brenda stifled a sob as Rita slid a thin arm around her shoulder. "Brenda, he can't get away with this—this libel. Or slander, or whatever it is. It's just plain wrong to write garbage like this about people."

Brenda was trembling, overwhelmed with embarrassment and shame. But she wouldn't allow herself the luxury of tears. Not here in the office with a full day of work ahead. And certainly not when Parnell could walk in at any minute.

Rita moved toward the doorway that led into the pharmacy. "I'll take care of the customers, Brenda. You take all the time you need." Slipping out, she quietly pulled the door closed behind her.

Brenda sat, staring at the newspaper in her hand. Her office with its pretty wicker shelves, gleaming white counter, and row upon row of bottles and canisters suddenly seemed unreal. Everything seemed to recede, leaving her in a timeless void, alone except for this photograph in front of her—accusing her.

How could she expect Parnell to forgive her for hurting him like this? What right had she to expect his understanding now? Had she killed their love? Maybe their relationship was as dead as her reputation would be when the residents of Columbia finished reading today's paper.

Brenda glanced out the window at the rain-slick cars jamming the parking lot. The pre-Christmas rush was in full swing, but Grinch O'Reilly had stolen all yuletide joy from her season. And for what? So he could get a scoop, a thrilling tidbit to entertain his readership and build his ratings and reputation.

May God forgive him. Brenda leaned forward and thrust her head into her hands. She tried to imagine her own reaction if she'd been in Parnell's place outside the courthouse yesterday, but she couldn't imagine anything beyond hitting a brick wall of shock. *Oh, Parnell, my love, what have I done?*

Later that afternoon, Brenda tried to telephone Parnell at his office and his home, but she kept getting his answering machine at
both places. When she talked to his secretary, the woman stone-
walled, saying Parnell was unavailable. He didn't return her calls.
He didn't drop by the pharmacy. No fresh roses arrived to replace
the ones that were beginning to wilt. When his green Jaguar was
missing from its reserved space for the second day running, Brenda
checked the back parking lot. The fact that Parnell had parked
there and used the rear entrance to the medical center, which allowed him to come and go without passing her glass-walled pharmacy, reinforced Brenda's conclusion. He was definitely avoid-
ing her.

She didn't dare try to contact him again, believing that to ini-
tiate contact would only make things worse. . .if that were possible. Instead, she waited and prayed and kept busy. Neither
Rita nor Tori asked questions, but kept a respectful distance. Several customers remarked on O'Reilly's article, calling it scandal-
ous, despicable, rude, and worse. But Brenda took little comfort
in their show of support. The one person whose support she needed
had chosen to remain silent.

Each empty day limped torturously into the next. Parnell didn't
show up at church or Bible study. He didn't ask her to help deliver toys to the Salvation Army. Brenda worked late each night
and went home to a solitary, micro-waved TV dinner. But Louise
called each evening to ask how she was doing.

"Mother, are these personal or professional telephone calls?"

Louise responded with a good-natured chuckle. "Perhaps a little
of each."

"Well. . .whatever. . .I do appreciate your calling. During the
day, staying busy helps crowd out the hurt and confusion. But
evenings are not so easy."

"That's what I thought, darling. We women need to process
our stress through talk, while men are more likely to retreat into
their caves. Just as Parnell is doing."

Brenda carried her cordless telephone over to her couch, plonked
down wearily, and propped her feet up on the antique walnut foot-

stool Louise had purchased for her during one of her many antiquing expeditions. "Caves? OK, Mom, what's that?"

"Well, darling, in the Indian—oops, I mean Native American—tradition, when something was bothering a brave, the young man would literally go into a cave and not emerge again until he'd solved his problem. No one, especially his wife, was allowed to follow him. In fact, his squaw was told that if she did go into the cave, a dragon would breathe fire on her!"

"Uh-hum. Fire-breathing dragons. Grumpy cavemen. I think I'm getting it. Go on."

"You see, that culture understood the masculine approach to dealing with stress. A man needs space and time to mull over what's troubling him. Only after he understands will he feel like talking. A woman, on the other hand, may react to stress by needing to talk in order to sort out her thoughts and feelings."

Brenda crossed her feet on the footstool and dangled one fur-lined slipper. "So you're telling me that Parnell has gone into an emotional hideout, and he's not coming out until he's good and ready?"

"Something like that. I know it's a difficult time for you, but for right now, sit tight and try to understand that this is his way of dealing with pain and frustration. It's not a rejection of you."

Brenda's hand tightened around the receiver. Her slipper tumbled to the floor. "Mom, it's not that I don't believe you—but this sure feels like rejection. He even uses the back door at the medical center so he doesn't have to see me!"

"I know it hurts, darling. But it sounds to me like the classic male response to stress. Try to appreciate the fact that Parnell cares enough to try to solve the problem—even if he's working it out alone in his cave."

Brenda sighed. "All right, I'll try, Mom. But this waiting is getting pretty lonely."

Louise chuckled. "Believe me, I know. Don't think your dear father hasn't taken a few trips into his cave over the years. Be wise and wait. Don't try to drag him out before he's ready, or you may run smack dab into a fire-breathing dragon!"

Parnell walked along the Mall in downtown Washington, D. C. His shoulders were hunched against the cold, his hands buried in his pockets, his feet crunching the thin layer of icy snow on the sidewalk. Christmas lights twinkled from street lamps and many of the windows of the government office buildings, but Parnell didn't notice.

He'd been walking the city streets for over an hour, trying to come to terms with what he'd recently learned. In his mind, he replayed Brenda's words, over and over, trying to let the reality of her story sink through his shock. She'd had a child—a daughter—born into shame and poverty despite Brenda's comfortable, middle-class background. After living through horrendous times, she'd decided to give up that daughter to adoption. Brenda hadn't been much more than a child herself, but she'd been wise enough to know that her baby needed a father as well as a mother.

Still. . .she'd kept all this a secret from him! That rankled Parnell. Why didn't she tell him? Didn't she trust him? The thought of her hiding things from him tore at his heart. Feelings of betrayal, bewilderment, and hurt rolled together into a hard, heavy lump in his chest.

At first, he'd been furious! Enfuriated by the humiliation dished out by a lowlife like Randy O'Reilly. Boy, did that smart! Parnell knew he was already in the public eye because of his progressive housing ideas, and he also knew that like parasites, O'Reilly and his ilk wouldn't pass up the opportunity to capitalize on his name. Their kind of gossip-mongering journalism reminded Parnell of looting.

He moved briskly and aggressively, ignoring the historic landmarks he passed, sparing only the briefest of glances at the huge, brightly-lit Christmas tree outside the White House. He walked and walked and walked, until he'd worked off his anger and his mind was clear. In that clarity, he saw Brenda—a lost, lonely, sick teenager who'd done the best she could. Courageous. Always courageous, except that she hadn't been able to muster the courage to tell him about her past.

So what? Parnell stopped and looked up at the crisp, white stars. *So what? She's not perfect. Neither are you, bud! She needs your forgiveness, not your condemnation.*

Parnell snapped his long, lean body around and headed back toward the car. After several blocks, he broke out into a jog. He had to find Brenda and explain. Had to make her understand why he'd left earlier. No doubt she blamed herself for everything. Maybe she even thought things were over between them. *Dear Lord, show me what to do, what to say. And. . .please. . .don't let me be too late!*

As he ran, he remembered his harsh comment about adoption during their dinner at the Baltimore Harbor. *Idiot! She was probably gearing up to tell you, and you scared her off with your precious opinions!*

Parnell drove fast and got back to his house outside Columbia in just less than thirty-five minutes, a new record, even in the Jaguar. He'd already decided it would be best not to just show up on Brenda's doorstep. After his abrupt departure, she deserved the courtesy of a telephone call first. She might not want to see a blundering oaf like him right now. *What was I thinking to give her the cold shoulder like that? When will I learn not to give in to the brooding Son of Thunder?*

Parnell burst into the house and gave a quick nod to Mrs. Crebs. She sat knitting in the living room as she usually did after putting Angelo to sleep. He went directly to the kitchen phone and was just about to grab the receiver when it rang.

"Is this the Mr. Pierce who was featured on the evening news tonight?"

Great, the prank calls begin. "Yes. Who is this?"

Twenty minutes later, Parnell put down the phone. He stood at the window, ramrod straight, stunned beyond belief. The stars, so bright and clear in the city, looked dull and lifeless. Despite the heat in the house, a lonely cold seeped into his bones. His stomach trembled. He massaged his temples to ease the dull ache that began to burn behind his eyes.

In the space of those few minutes, everything had changed.

nine

Brenda didn't hear from Parnell again until after Gil Montgomery's guilty verdict had been announced on the evening news, a full eight days after her court appearance. After her testimony, the defense attorneys had spent four days parading their expert witnesses, and the jury had taken another four to deliberate.

She sat perched on the edge of the couch in her living room in front of the TV, her hands clenched in her lap as she watched a sullen Montgomery being led away. *Thank God. Justice has been done.*

When her phone rang, she nearly didn't answer it. All day long, reporters had been hounding her at the pharmacy. It had gotten so bad, she'd stopped taking calls. But so far, they hadn't bothered her at home, probably thanks to her unlisted number.

"Hello?" she asked tentatively, fully prepared to say she wasn't giving any comments.

"Brenda. . .this is Parnell."

"Oh. . ." *Did he have to introduce himself? Does he think I don't remember the sound of his voice?* Gil Montgomery disappeared from the TV only to be replaced by an advertisement for laundry detergent. Brenda clicked the remote and the screen went dark.

She had the feeling the brave was about to come out of his cave.

"Uh. . .seems you left your red gloves in my car," he began.

Brenda felt a wave of compassion when she heard the nervousness in his tone. "I was wondering where I'd left them," she said, knowing full well this call wasn't about her gloves. "Did you see the Montgomery verdict?"

"Yes. It appears that justice has been served—this time, at least."

"Thank God! Oh, Parnell. . .it's so good to hear your voice

again."

The line went silent for a few moments. "Look, Brenda, I'm sorry I've been acting like a jerk. The whole baby thing was. . .a shock. . ."

Brenda let out the breath that had gotten stuck in her chest. This call was going better than she'd dared hope. She saw an opening for reconciliation and dove for it. "Kind of like the shock of sitting on a barrel of gunpowder when it explodes?"

"Yeah, you might say that."

"And the fuse was lit by O'Reilly. . .and me."

Parnell cleared his throat. "O'Reilly's hated me since high school."

"Oh? I didn't know the two of you went back that far."

"I was the preacher's kid, working with Christian groups during the summers to build houses for the poor. O'Reilly was the class Communist, preaching that the poor could only be helped through political ideology, not charity. He's been nipping at my heels ever since. I think he was using you to get at me."

"Maybe so. . .but I never should have put you in that position. He certainly got his scoop—at our expense. I'm so sorry, Parnell."

"So am I."

"No, what I mean is, I'm sorry I gave O'Reilly the opportunity to ambush you. If I'd told you about the baby. . ." Her words petered out into silence. She twisted the telephone cord around her finger, waiting for his response.

Finally, he cleared his throat. "Were you planning to tell me?"

"Y—yes, I was. I tried to. I really did. . .the evening we had dinner at that seafood restaurant in Baltimore. I wanted to, but. . ."

"But what?"

"Well, you seemed so negative about adoption and. . .and unsure about abortion. I was afraid you wouldn't understand, especially about giving her up after eleven months. . ."

More silence. Brenda wound the cord so tightly, it cut off the blood supply. Her forefinger started to turn blue.

Finally, Parnell spoke. From the strained timbre of his voice, Brenda could tell this wasn't easy for him. "Brenda, can we just forget all this? It's in the past now. O'Reilly's column will blow over. He'll be exploiting someone else tomorrow. Let's pretend this fiasco never happened and just get on with our lives. After all, it's nearly Angelo's birthday."

Brenda hauled in a shaky breath and let the rubbery plastic telephone cord unwind itself from her finger. This wasn't the answer she'd hoped for. It was too abrupt, too easy. She wanted to talk, to communicate, to get to the bottom of things. But it was obvious that Parnell wasn't ready to do that yet. Her mom was right. The brave would talk only when he was ready. *OK, Parnell, I'll go along with you. I'll take whatever crumbs you throw me. And I'll wait. . .*

"If that's what you want. . ."

"What I want," he said, "is for things to be the way they were. Before O'Reilly's bomb."

Brenda bit her lip. "Parnell, I want you back. . .I don't want this to come between us. Our love is too precious."

"So you'll be at the bowling alley for Angelo's party?"

Brenda smiled at the anticipation of the small boy's happiness. He'd been planning this party for months. "You bet. I wouldn't miss my future stepson's party for the world."

❧

Inside Bowl-A-Rama, the lights were low and the noise level high. The clattering of tumbling bowling pins was ever-present, like the crashing of waves on the beach. The lanes gleamed, and the computerized bowling stations were state-of-the-art. Overhead, the electronic scoring board enthralled several of the more gadget-minded children in Angelo's group.

A dozen six-, seven- and eight-year-olds, mostly boys, played on the two end lanes, which were lined along the gutters with gaily colored bumpers. These bumpers were designed to thwart wayward balls and coax them along to their final destination. Brenda watched, with bemused delight, as each child took his turn.

One redheaded boy swung his ball half a dozen times before throwing. Angelo, dressed in black pants and a red and green rugby shirt, did a little dance each time he let go of his ball. Each child, except for Amanda, whose father played in a bowling league, plonked the ball onto the lane with a ceremonious, loud thud rather than rolling it smoothly. Had it not been for the bumpers, the gutter balls would have outnumbered the strikes, spares, or any other direct contact with the pins.

"What does it matter?" Brenda whispered across the scoring desk to Parnell. "At least they're having fun."

"Right," Parnell replied, fiddling with the automatic scoring that seemed to have suddenly gone haywire. He gave her a quick, tight smile.

He's trying so hard, she thought, looking away in dismay. *But it sure looks like work.*

"Daddy! Daddy! I knocked down seven pins!" screeched Angelo as he ran and hugged his father's neck. "Seven! That's how old I am!"

It seemed to Brenda that Parnell had to make a tremendous effort to rise to his son's enthusiasm. "Seven pins! What a big boy! I'm so proud of you!" he said as he tussled Angelo's wavy black hair. After enduring about ten seconds of paternal endearment, the boy wriggled free and skipped over to his friends. Parnell's smile faded.

When Angelo looked back, Parnell brightened up again, but when he wasn't in the spotlight, his spirits sagged and he stared silently down the bowling lane. His long, lean frame slumped in the brown plastic chair and he looked oddly out of place, a dark, brooding figure in the middle of the gaiety of a child's party.

Brenda checked her impulse to slide her arm around his shoulders and ask what was wrong. *He'll tell you when he's ready. Let him stay in his cave as long as he needs to.* Even so, it tore at her heart to see him like this, so miserable and so determined to hide it. She said a quick prayer that the Holy Spirt would comfort him.

Brenda stood up and wandered over to the glassed-in eating area directly behind the bowlers' chairs. She chatted with several of the children's parents as they drank coffee and listened to a football game on the overhead TV. Two of the mothers helped her set out paper plates for ice-cream cake. While Brenda filled cups with Coke, she stole a glance at Parnell. He sat, elbows on the scoring table, his hands thrust through his thick black hair, his yellow cotton pullover strained across his broad shoulders.

He needs time, and I need to respect that. He'll be back. . .I think. Shaking off the troubling thought, she busied herself playing master of ceremonies, corralling the children to the table, leading the singing, dishing out treats, overseeing the gift opening. Before long, Parnell rose to the occasion and joined the party. He seemed to come out of himself as he cut the cake, cheered when Angelo blew out his candles, and generally put up a good show of merriment for the children.

But as the party progressed and the children returned to bowling after demolishing the birthday cake, Parnell sank back into his brooding like an anchor sinking to the bottom of the sea. Brenda found it harder and harder to feel cheerful and play the role of the happy hostess. She tried to talk to Parnell, even linking arms with him once. It almost seemed as if he wanted to talk, but couldn't quite bring himself to pull it off. He mumbled monosyllabic answers and didn't even seem to notice when she withdrew her arm.

Brenda tried not to take his mood personally, but his heaviness began to rub off on her, draining her energy and good spirits. The clatter of falling bowling pins and the laughter and shrieks of the children started to give her a headache. But she smiled, nodded, and clapped and kept up appearances, all the while hoping the party would be over soon.

At last, the parents began arriving to pick up their children. "What's wrong with my daddy?" Angelo whispered to Brenda as his friends were being bundled into coats and snowsuits.

"What makes you think there's something wrong?" *Kids! They don't miss a thing!*

"Oh, I dunno. It's like he's only pretending to have fun. After my mommy went to heaven, Daddy used to be like that. But then he met you and he was happy again for real. I can tell."

"I'm sure you can, Angelo."

Brenda looked over at Parnell who was picking up discarded wrapping paper and loading presents into a large cardboard box. A weariness clung to him, a blackness she couldn't name.

"Why isn't Daddy happy now, Brenda?"

"I'm—I'm not sure, honey," she said, hugging Angelo. "Maybe he's not feeling well."

"Like when my tummy used to hurt?"

"Something like that." Brenda's heart melted. She dropped down on one knee and drew Angelo close. The boy relaxed into her embrace. "I love you, sweetheart."

"I love you, too."

He hugged her quickly before trotting off to say goodbye to the last few stragglers.

If only I could ease Parnell's hurts as easily, she thought miserably.

❧

Brenda had been anticipating spending the week between Angelo's birthday and Christmas in Parnell's company. She had so looked forward to shopping, gift-wrapping, looking at lights—all the holiday festivities she'd loved since childhood—with her husband-to-be. But she hadn't seen Parnell once since the birthday party. That had been five days ago. Once again, he seemed to be boycotting the pharmacy. His few phone calls were stilted and awkward to the point of being embarrassing.

Twice she blew her good intention of waiting outside the cave—like the Indian squaw—and asked what was wrong. "Nothing," was all he'd say.

But Brenda wasn't buying it. Something was terribly wrong. Like grains of sand slipping through her fingers, she could feel Parnell distancing himself emotionally. The worst part was, she didn't know why, and it seemed that he couldn't tell her. But she could see his suffering. She ached to comfort him, but he wouldn't—or couldn't—confide in her. He had slipped beyond her reach, and she was helpless to bring him back.

The season's first snowfall only exacerbated her feelings of isolation. But at least the last-minute Christmas rush at the pharmacy served as a distraction, and for that she was grateful. One particularly vexing problem occupied her for days. A family from church was visiting a missionary in a South American jungle. They needed to protect their toddler from diarrhea, but they couldn't carry gallons of Pedialite. It took Brenda several experiments and a call to the compounding school in Texas to come up with a powder that could do the job when reconstituted with water.

If Parnell didn't telephone, at least Louise did. "Sounds like Parnell may be depressed," her mother remarked during a late afternoon call. "Remember, he lost his wife and parents only two years ago. Christmas must be particularly rough for him."

"Of course, Mom. Why didn't I think of that?" She paused. "But I think this is more than holiday blues. I'm afraid I'm losing him."

"Really? I didn't know things were that serious."

Brenda sighed as she switched the telephone receiver to her other ear. She checked to make sure Tori was out in the pharmacy, stocking shelves, away from earshot. Brenda didn't like conducting such intensely personal conversations at work, but she desperately needed her mother's advice. "I don't know how or why, but Parnell started to pull away from me the day of O'Reilly's interview."

"Did you and he discuss how the media exposure could affect your relationship?"

Brenda felt a lump forming in her throat. "Well, kind of. He called and admitted that learning about the baby was a shock. Then he apologized for acting like a jerk and said he wanted to forget the whole thing. . .just take up where we left off and pretend it never happened."

"Just pretend?" Louise Ford raised her well-modulated voice a notch or two. "Someone needs to tell this man that denial is not a river in Egypt."

"Right."

"Sweeping things under the rug never works."

Suddenly, tears welled up in Brenda's eyes. She was glad no

customers were around. "No, it didn't. Parnell tried to be cheerful at Angelo's birthday party, but it was painfully obvious to me that it was an act. Emotionally, I can't reach him."

Louise paused. "Did you ask him what was wrong?"

"Oh, Mom! I asked him several times, pleaded with him. He either won't, or can't tell me."

"Darling, my guess is it's the latter. My advice is to hang in there. Love is patient. He'll tell you in his own time."

Several times a day, Brenda prayed for patience, kindness, and love. She also prayed for endurance. Parnell's silence had become a sheer stone cliff she couldn't scale. *He'll come out of his cave,* she kept telling herself. *Don't give up hope.*

❧

When Parnell telephoned the pharmacy on December 23 and confirmed their date to worship together at the candlelight Christmas Eve service, Brenda dared hope that maybe he was ready to emerge. She spent hours choosing a Christmas outfit at Columbia Mall, finally deciding on a classic cashmere two-piece, all green and red and glittery, with black patent leather pumps and black stockings. That evening, she pulled her blond hair up into a topknot, securing the braid with a large, ornate gold clip Parnell had given her. She dabbed a light, floral perfume on her neck and wrists, slipped into her new green suede coat complete with a holly wreath pin on the lapel, and sat on the living room window seat and waited.

The hands on the grandfather clock in the corner moved relentlessly forward. Eleven o'clock chimed. Then a quarter past eleven. The service, or at least the ecumenical caroling program, would begin in fifteen minutes. Brenda twisted the strap of her leather shoulder purse. Fifteen minutes to go. Fourteen. Hope was fast melting into irritation.

She opened her purse and closed her hand around her car keys. The church was only a five-minute drive away. If Parnell didn't have the decency to pick her up on time. . .well, she'd just drive herself. She was getting mighty tired of being treated like yesterday's newspaper.

Just then Parnell's dark green Jaguar pulled into her driveway.

Not waiting for him to ring the bell, Brenda snapped off the lamp, let herself out the front door, and stepped into the chilly night air. Parnell, wearing a tailored gray wool coat, unfolded his long lean frame from the low-slung vehicle. "Sorry I'm late, Brenda," he said, spreading his black gloved hands. "An emergency with one of my tenants."

Brenda saw the sincerity on his face, as well as an indefinable sadness. Something about the weary slump of his shoulders touched her. She bit back her irritation and forced herself to practice the virtue of cheerfulness instead. "No problem," she said as he held the car door open for her.

She slid into the soft leather seat and waited for him to join her on the other side. "Looks like we might have a white Christmas after all," she chatted, trying to lighten his mood.

Parnell grunted and put the key in the ignition.

Brenda had hoped he might comment on her appearance, but he didn't. He backed up and started down the road without a word, barely noticing her, never mind complimenting her new hairstyle and outfit. Without taking his eyes off the road, he reached over to the dashboard and clicked on the radio.

Christmas music had never sounded so hauntingly lonely, Brenda thought. She tried to ignore the headache starting at the base of her skull as her irritation gave way to disappointment. The further they drove, the more desolate she felt.

"Where's Angelo?" she asked, more determined than ever to draw Parnell out of himself and his doldrums.

"With his Sunday school class," Parnell answered, his voice dull. "He's part of the children's choir tonight. The director called at the last minute."

"That's wonderful, but he's going to be tired after such a late night." Now she was scrambling to make conversation.

He shrugged. "I guess."

Brenda felt her stomach tying in knots. Parnell's mood hung like a dark cloud over the atmosphere, suffocating her, chilling the blood in her veins. For the rest of the trip, only the sounds of Dean Martin's "White Christmas" broke the silence.

ten

Hundreds of worshipers milled around the lobby of the Columbia Interfaith Center. Six Christian denominations shared the single-level, rambling, stone-and-brick building. Each denomination retained its own integrity, while at the same time interacting with other churches. Several interfaith centers just like this one were scattered across Columbia. The designers of the planned city saw them as a means to save community resources while encouraging ecumenism.

Tonight, Brenda noticed that the huge lobby felt pleasantly warm. The air was heavy with the scent of pine and a wood-burning fire, and the atmosphere was thick with swirls of colorful clothing, snatches of gaiety, cheerful exchanges of Christmas greetings. In each corner stood a tall, trimmed tree, complete with golden stars and angels clad in flowing, white chiffon.

Although it was 11:30, time for the caroling program to start, people were still drifting in from the parking lot, stamping their feet and rubbing their hands. A cold gust of wind ushered in every new group each time the huge glass doors opened. At the far end of the rustic redwood area, about one hundred children stood on temporary bleachers placed on both sides of the enormous stone fireplace. The flames crackled orange and yellow, devouring the wood, sending sparks shooting up the chimney like stars trying to leap back into the black velvet sky.

Yes, it's Christmas, Brenda mused. Despite Parnell's moodiness, she had much to rejoice about. This caroling choir, for one. The children came from various ethnic and denominational backgrounds, reflecting the cultural diversity of Columbia. Despite differences in doctrine or race, they were assembled for one reason and one reason only: to praise the Prince of Peace.

Three generations back, Brenda's family had immigrated from Ireland with stories of bitterness and bloodshed among Christians in that war-torn land. Brenda wished those forefathers and mothers could see how times had changed, at least in Columbia, Maryland. Here different branches of the Lord's family came together in worship instead of bombing and maiming each other.

To be sure, many divisions were still unhealed, she knew, but at least Christians were making a joyful noise unto their Lord together. Brenda smiled wistfully as she recalled one of her Grandma Ford's favorite sayings regarding the broken body of Christian believers: "In essentials, unity; in nonessentials, diversity; in all things, charity."

Brenda's attention focused on the choir director, a big-boned black woman in a brilliant, flowing African robe. She noticed the woman had arranged the children according to height rather than denomination. Baptists stood alongside Catholics; Methodists rubbed shoulders with Lutherans, Presbyterians with nondenominationals. At her signal, the children's voices rose and blended into one glorious song announcing the birth of their one Savior.

Brenda and Parnell stood as near to the choir as the crowd would allow. Brenda could hear Angelo belt out his favorite carol, "Hark the Herald Angels Sing," with enough gusto for half-a-dozen seven-year-old boys. The crowd was thick, pressing in, and Brenda inched closer to Parnell. How she loved Christmas, the season of hope that with God all things were possible! The glorious impossible had already happened in Bethlehem. The Incarnation was a miracle of impossible love, she mused, the love of the Creator for His creatures. And like love, it could not be explained, only believed in and rejoiced over.

Brenda sighed happily and indulged herself by resting her head against Parnell's shoulder. She could feel the softness of his overcoat against her cheek. She fully expected him to slide his arm around her and pull her closer, as he'd done a thousand times before. But he didn't. He stood stiff as the Christmas trees in the corners. He didn't look at her, but stared straight ahead, his dark eyes fixed on his son.

Her joy disintegrated like a cloud of breath in frosty air. To save face, she lifted her head and rummaged through her purse on the pretext of looking for a tissue. After dabbing at her nose, she stood at attention, inwardly hurting but determined to ignore Parnell's coldness with all the dignity she could muster. She didn't touch him again, acutely aware of his stony standoffishness.

After twenty minutes of enthusiastic singing and a particularly moving rendition of "O, Little Town of Bethlehem," the director dismissed the children and Angelo hurled himself through the throng and flung his arms around Parnell. "Did I do good, Dad?" he demanded, breathless.

Parnell smiled stiffly. "You did great, son."

Angelo flashed his brown puppy-dog eyes at Brenda. "Did'ja like it?"

Brenda rubbed Angelo's dark curls. "I can't remember ever hearing such good Christmas singing," she said as they began to walk toward the room assigned to Covenant Community Church. Each denomination used a different room of the large building as their worship sanctuary.

"For real?"

"Honest, cross my heart." She gave him an affectionate squeeze. She wasn't going to let any chilliness between her and Parnell ruin Angelo's Christmas. She kept her hand on the boy's shoulder as they navigated their way through the jostling crowd. As they stepped into Covenant's room, buzzing with Christmas chatter, Brenda busied herself looking for three seats near the front.

"There!" she cried, hurrying ahead. As they settled in, she avoided making eye contact with Parnell and tried to ignore the fact he didn't offer to help her with her coat. Angelo sat between them, perched on the edge of the padded, foldout chair. Brenda looked around. She recalled her initial dismay at the spartan modernness of Covenant Community Church's worship area when her niece first invited her to attend services here. That was two years ago, when Brenda had first moved to Columbia.

The rustic room fringed with potted plants and hanging ferns looked more like the lobby of a ski resort than the sanctuary of a church. There was no stained glass, no cross, no pulpit, no organ. Just a large space done in earth tones, with a wooden table up front that served as an altar. The churches using the room furnished their own accessories. As a newcomer to the interfaith concept, it had all seemed strange to Brenda, but after a while she found herself agreeing with Tori that such plain worship held few distractions and emphasized the church as people rather than buildings.

But tonight was different. The room was aglow with scores of candles flickering against hundreds of red poinsettias spiraling upward in the shape of a Christmas tree behind the altar. To the right stood a large, life-size creche, complete with straw and electrically-powered star over the stable. Mary and Joseph looked down tenderly and protectively at their divine charge.

"Can you see the baby Jesus?" Brenda leaned over and whispered to Angelo.

The boy pulled himself up and strained to see over the hats and hairdos. "Yes! I can see Him!"

"Isn't the creche beautiful?"

"Oh, yes," he said, the tone of his young voice full of awe and reverence. "It's the most coolest thing in the world."

Brenda smiled at his choice of words. For elementary school kids in the nineties, "cool" was the highest praise possible. She continued admiring the creche and found her focus drawn not to the Baby or his mother, but to the actual manger itself. It had been crafted of bleached, hand-hewn oak, and the surface of the planks clearly showed the scars of the rough implements used to shape them.

For the first time, Brenda connected the wood of the cradle of Bethlehem with the wood of the cross of Calvary. Christ's redemptive suffering had begun long before Golgotha, she realized.

As she meditated on this insight, devotion and love swelled in her heart, and, for the moment, the pain of Parnell's despondency was eclipsed with joy.

Just then, Pastor Milligan and the cross-bearer processed in. The pastor was a lean, middle-aged man with thick, steel-rimmed glasses and all the body movements of a bifocal wearer. Brenda liked his insightful sermons, his Christlike kindness, and his knack for saying the right thing to someone who was hurting.

As she was hurting now.

She stole a sidelong glance at Parnell. He was singing forcefully, holding the purple hymnal tightly, but she sensed a heaviness about him, a melancholia. She wanted nothing more than to hold and comfort him. *Why can't he open up to me? I love him so much. Have I caused this breach? If so, I wonder if he'll ever trust me again.* Blinking back tears, she tried to sing, but, afraid that her voice would crack, ended up mouthing the words.

Out of the corner of her eye, she caught sight of her sister, Marcie, with her husband, Barry, and their four children sitting three rows ahead over in the next aisle. Marcie didn't see her, but Brenda breathed a sigh of relief. At least she had family here tonight.

Brenda's concentration, in addition to her nerves, was shot. She found herself tuning in and out during the entire service. Pastor Milligan preached a powerful sermon on hope, but she missed most of it. She caught bits and pieces, something about the hopes and fears of all the years meeting in Christ. "We cling to the hope given us in the revelation of Christmas—that our God is with us," she heard him say. "As a result, we can have hope enough to meet all our fears. Beloved, we have barely begun to plumb the depths of this mystery of Hope."

It was then Brenda became aware of her own fears and lack of hope. The irritation, the disappointment, the anger. . .they all sprang from lack of hope, which was firmly rooted in fear. Fear. She contemplated the word. Yes, the underlying emotion was fear.

But fear of what?

She wanted to know, but. . .she didn't want to know. To put her fear into words might make it real, might bring it to pass.

Then the truth broke through, sending cracks shooting through Brenda's protective shield as surely as the roots of a tree shoot cracks through the sidewalk. *I'm afraid of losing Parnell.* Or to put it more accurately, she was afraid Parnell was going to leave her, driven away by her betrayal of their love.

Hadn't that been her fear all along? Wasn't that why she had hesitated to confide in him earlier, as her mother had urged her to do? Wasn't she more like Rita Andreas than she cared to admit? Afraid of losing her man if she did the right thing?

Oh, Lord! Lord!

The realization hit her with the force of one of those steam engines Angelo so loved to ride. She fumbled with her hymnal, looking in vain for the next hymn, gave up, and closed her eyes. *Dear Jesus,* she prayed, *deliver me from all my fears. Fear is not of You, Lord. Make Your perfect love cast out my fear. I trust You. My life, my problems, even my fears, I commit into Your hands.*

Emotionally, she felt no better after her prayer, but she believed God had heard her nonetheless. After the service, Brenda caught Marcie's eye over the crowd and signaled that they'd meet out in the lobby. Parnell didn't say a word or touch her as they stood in line to shake the minister's hand.

"Ah, Brenda," said Pastor Milligan, taking her hand in both of his and clasping it. "I'm so sorry to hear that you've become the latest victim of our gossip-mad media. So sorry. But remember that Christ was also mocked in His lifetime, and that He bore it patiently and humbly, giving us an example to follow. God will vindicate you."

"Thank you," said Brenda softly, taken by surprise and moved by his insight.

"You did the right thing all those years ago," Pastor Milligan continued, "and don't let anyone else tell you otherwise. We're all behind you, my dear."

With a final squeeze, he released her hand and moved on to the next person. Brenda realized that the condemnation she'd been expecting as fallout from the media circus simply hadn't materialized. If anything, people had made a point of voicing their support.

But something had happened on the day of the courthouse fiasco that had changed—damaged—her relationship with Parnell, perhaps irrevocably. The day that disaster had befallen her in the form of Randy O'Reilly.

"Brenda! Brenda!" Angelo called, tugging at her sleeve. "There's Aunt Marcie and Brian." He pointed toward the stone fireplace where Marcie stood with her eight-year-old twins, Betty and Brian.

"Let's go say hello." Brenda took Angelo's arm. She looked around to ask Parnell to accompany them and stopped dead in her tracks. His face had turned ashen. His pained expression alarmed her.

"Parnell! Wha—what's the matter?"

"We've got to talk, and we've got to talk now," he said, his voice low and urgent. "Alone. Outside."

"OK," she said, taken aback. "I'll see if Marcie can watch Angelo."

She'd barely finished her sentence before Parnell turned and walked toward the glass doors leading to the parking lot, his broad shoulders slumped, his hands thrust deep in his pockets.

"What's wrong with Daddy? He looked funny."

Brenda pulled Angelo closer as they maneuvered through the crowd. "I don't know, sweetheart. But he and I need to have a little, grown-up talk. Will you stay with Aunt Marcie for a little while?"

"I can play with Brian? Cool!"

Brenda offered a silent prayer of thanksgiving for the emotional resiliency of children and waved to her sister. Marcie stood beside the great stone fireplace, one hand on the head of each towheaded twin. Ten years her senior, Marcie looked like an older, more matronly version of Brenda. Her figure was heavier, her jaw squarer, but the golden hair and full red lips were the same.

"Marcie, help!"

"My goodness." Marcie laid a plump hand on Brenda's forearm. "What on earth is wrong with Parnell? He looks like his dog just died!"

"Daddy doesn't have a dog!" put in Angelo.

"I know, sweetheart," said Brenda, tossing his hair a little. "Aunt Marcie's just teasing. It's just a way of saying that your daddy looks sad, like he'd look if he had a dog that died."

"Oh!" Immediately, Angelo and the twins began making plans for a game of tag.

"Marcie, could Angelo stay with you a few minutes? Parnell wants...a grown-up chat."

Marcie's kind face creased into a smile. "Sure thing, little sister. And don't forget, you and I can have a 'grown-up chat' later, if you need it. By the way, I like your hair. Great outfit!"

"Thanks," murmured Brenda, pulling on her suede coat as she headed toward the door, her heart heavy. *Hope, Brenda. Hang on to hope. God's still in control.*

Outside, Parnell was waiting for her, the collar of his overcoat turned up against the biting cold wind. Already a few white flakes were drifting down. As soon as Brenda stepped through the glass doors, he stepped forward and touched her arm. "Let's talk in the car," he muttered.

Perhaps it was Pastor Milligan's sermon—or at least the parts she'd heard—that gave her courage. Or maybe she was just sick and tired of waiting outside the cave. She was going to confront him and get answers. She had to. She couldn't go on like this, feeling rejected, unloved, ashamed. She thrust her hands into her pockets, ruing the fact that she'd forgotten her gloves. She'd been so irritated with Parnell earlier, she'd left them on the couch back home.

They crossed the parking lot in silence, a frosty white light from the half-moon doing little to dispel the inky blackness. Fingers of cold slithered down Brenda's neck and she turned up her coat collar. The vapor lights cast haloes against the blacktop. The first fat flakes of an approaching snowstorm floated before the round globes of light, distorting their pale yellow glow.

Since they'd arrived late to the service, the Jaguar was parked half a mile up the road, far from the full parking lot. Parnell was walking so fast, Brenda's legs screamed in protest as she took longer and longer strides to keep up.

"Hey! Slow down!" she gasped.

He stopped and turned to her. "I'm sorry. I didn't realize I was walking so fast."

They resumed at a slower pace, walking uphill toward the car. Brenda listened to the snow crackle beneath their feet and the sound of Parnell's breathing cutting through the crisp, brittle night. They walked past house after house strung with Christmas lights and decorations, the festiveness mocking their gloomy silence. Brenda searched for something to say to break the ice.

"You've been very quiet lately, Parnell." *That's an understatement, but at least it's a start.*

He grunted. "I've had a lot on my mind. I've been thinking. . . evaluating. . ."

"Evaluating. . .me?"

"No. I've been thinking about life and all the surprises that can yank the rug from under you. . .and how sometimes things aren't what they seem."

Oh, great. You're talking about Randy O'Reilly's little revelation, aren't you? I'm not what I seemed to be. Well, why don't you just come out and say so?

He stared off into the distance and didn't say anymore. The stars looked pale and remote by the light of the slice of moon and Brenda wondered how much colder it could get in outer space. *Hope, Brenda. Remember. . .* But with each step, she felt more and more helpless in the face of Parnell's aloofness.

He's suffering. But I'm suffering, too. OK, it's now or never.

"I know something's troubling you, Parnell, and I want to help you, whatever it is. But you've got to tell me what you're thinking. I can't read your mind. And I can't go on like this."

He stopped, but looked down at the snowy ground. She reached out and touched his upper arm. He flinched. Hurt, she withdrew her hand as quickly as if she'd touched hot coals. When he still refused to face her, she walked around in front of him.

"Why are you shutting me out?"

"I'm not shutting you out. I just need time." He looked up then, and stared at her, pure misery in his eyes. He stood as straight and rigid as the nearby lamppost. Brenda could see his frustration as he clenched and unclenched his gloved hands.

Confusion and hurt formed a hard lump in her throat. "How long do you need, Parnell? Forever? Because, let me tell you, that's what it feels like."

She waited, her throat tightening. She studied him in the light of the street lamp. The lines etched across the planes of his face seemed to have deepened, as if they'd been cut into a crystal goblet by a master hand. Lines of pain, of struggle. She ached for him, but she couldn't reach him. The harder she tried, the more he pulled away.

A look of bewilderment crossed his dark features. Twice, he started to say something, but stopped. Finally, he shrugged his shoulders.

"What's wrong?" she said at last. "I want to be with you, whatever you're going through. For better or for worse. I'm going to be your wife, after all."

He closed his eyes and hauled in a ragged breath. Then he looked at her, spreading his hands in a helpless gesture. "I don't know how to explain. . .but things have changed for me."

"Changed? How?" A horrible fear grasped her like a giant hand and began squeezing. Her fears were coming to pass. She'd given her heart to this man; now she was afraid he was about to hand it back.

"I've been doing a lot of thinking, and. . .I'd like to postpone the wedding. . ."

His words seemed to ring through the empty night with the finality of gunshots. "Postpone. . .but why?"

"I can't explain. I don't completely understand myself. . ."

It was happening. He was leaving her, just as she'd feared. He was just letting her down slowly. Desperately, she tried to hang on. "Look, Parnell, I love you. I love you more than I thought it was possible to love someone, and it's because I love you that I want to work this out. What is it? The baby? The fact that I didn't tell you? That I betrayed you by keeping her a secret? What? Tell me!" She dragged in a deep, shuddering breath and struggled not to burst into tears.

"Something's happened. . ."

"But the wedding's only weeks away. . .the invitations. . ." Her heart raced. Was he getting ready to reject her once and for all? "We can't call everything off now!"

Parnell cleared his throat. He spoke slowly and deliberately, with authority in his voice. "We must. I need time. . ."

His adamancy pulled her up short. Then something inside Brenda snapped. She narrowed her eyes and put her fists on her hips. "You don't love me anymore, that's the real reason, isn't it? But you don't have the courage to admit it. We're just like that couple my Mom counseled. When the wife found out the husband kept a secret from her, she couldn't trust him anymore, so they split up. That's what's happening with us, isn't it? I've betrayed your trust. . .and you've fallen out of love with me!"

His face reflected the anguish she felt ripping through her own heart. He was a man at war with himself. He began to speak and his words tumbled over each other in a rush of exasperation. "I don't know what to say, Brenda. I don't know what the future's going to hold now. Everything has changed. Yes, it's about betrayal, and abandonment, and. . .but I haven't fallen out of love with you."

Despite the earnestness of his words, her own fear kept her from believing him. *This is the beginning of the end.* Tears blurred

Brenda's vision. Her head felt light; her knees, weak. What had begun as a trickle of apprehension was now a rushing river. She was slipping, losing control. She was losing him. She'd probably lost him already, from the moment O'Reilly exposed her in front of the courthouse.

She spun around on her heel, not wanting him to see her tears. She had her pride left, at least. Cold, lonely pride. The snow was coming down harder now, freezing the wetness on her cheeks. She lifted her hands to her face. Her skin was as cold as marble against her fingers. The diamond of her engagement ring glinted.

"Brenda, wait. . ."

"I'll get my own ride home. Take all the time you need. The rest of your life, for all I care!" Impulsively, she jerked her engagement ring off her finger, turned to him, and jammed the ring into his hand. He looked at her, open-mouthed.

She wasn't finished. "And you can take this, too." She reached up and pulled the gold hair clip out of her topknot and flung it to the ground. The dull, muffled sound of it hitting the snow seemed to fill the night.

Shaken to the core by the ferocity of her own emotions, she turned and ran in the direction of the interfaith center, her unbound hair tumbling down, her cheeks slick with tears, her hope gone. She fled, and never looked back to witness the despair on Parnell's face as he stood in the swirling snow with a ring in his hand and a golden hair clip at his feet, looking as desolate as an abandoned building.

eleven

Brenda stood alone at her mother's living room window, stealing a few quiet moments away from the Christmas Day bustle in the kitchen. She gazed out over the frozen lake behind her parents' property. The huge sheet of water looked like a white field. The second snowfall of the day sauntered down from the heavens in huge, heavy flakes. In the late afternoon light, the landscape looked soft and smudged, as if an artist had run his thumb over a charcoal sketch.

Over the clatter of pans and the electrical hum of the blender, she could hear Rochelle Jones and her three young boys laugh loudly at her father's jokes. Her mom's chortle at her dad's latest witticism echoed their merriment. Sharing Christmas with a homeless family was a tradition Brenda had always enjoyed, but not this Christmas. Her emotions were shot, pulled as tight as an overstrung violin. Her father's trademark booming laugh gave her a feeling of haunting sadness.

In fact, Brenda hadn't felt so detached from holiday festivities since her husband died five years previously. Today she just wanted to be alone, to brood over her breakup with Parnell. She'd tried to bow out of dinner, fearing that Parnell would show up as planned, but Louise wouldn't hear of it.

"I don't care if you two launched World War III last night," her mother had lectured over the telephone that morning. "You're not shutting out your family on Christmas Day!"

Unwillingly, she'd come, and so far, Parnell had failed to show up. Nor had he called. Brenda supposed she should be glad. At least she hadn't had to encounter her now ex-fiancé and feel pressured to put on a happy face in front of the guests. But in actuality, she felt more miserable than ever.

Her outburst at Parnell last night continued to amaze her. She'd lain awake all night, reliving the events. Had she really hurled those cruel barbs at the man she loved? Had she really given his ring back? Flung her hair clip on the ground? Brenda shook her head. How could she have been so insensitive, so hurtful? It was almost as if she'd panicked—so afraid that he was about to break their engagement that she'd wanted to beat him to the punch, to hurt him before he hurt her. She sighed. *And I dare call myself a Christian? Lord, help me!*

Brenda knew enough about human nature to realize that such sudden, explosive anger was rooted in emotional pain. Pain as deep as the Grand Canyon, maybe. She hadn't realized how severely Parnell's withdrawal had hurt her until she'd lashed out at him. *But hadn't he left me already in his heart? Wasn't I only putting the unspoken reality into words? Wasn't his asking for a postponement just a way of letting me down gently?*

That thought chilled her as much as the white landscape and desolate bare black trees huddling against the immense grayness of sky. The whole world looked deserted, she thought, in spite of the large, angular-style wooden homes clustered around the lake. There wasn't a human being—man, woman, or child—in sight. Not even a dog, or a bird.

Brenda wrapped her arms around herself. The outer world mirrored her inner bleakness. The wind gusted around the Fords' home, whipping up the snowflakes into blurry whirlwinds. The waist-high stone walls enclosing the Fords' yard, as well as the long, narrow lawn itself, were fast disappearing under a ghostly blanket.

The crystal clock on the mantelpiece chimed five o'clock. She hadn't heard from Parnell since she'd run away from him last night. Marcie had driven her home, without questions. Brenda had avoided saying good night to Angelo, relieved that he was too engrossed in playing with friends from Sunday school to notice her departure. Parnell and Angelo were supposed to join the Fords for Christmas Day dinner at six. And Parnell hadn't called to cancel, not yet anyway. Part of her dreaded seeing him; another, stronger part wanted to apologize for her behavior.

Lights began snapping on inside the houses around the lake. Brenda pictured happy families and couples sitting down to holiday tables, trading gifts and stories by the fire, children squealing as they ripped open brightly colored wrapping tissue, blond women being kissed under the mistletoe by tall, dark-haired men. . . *Oh, Lord, I really blew it this time! You gave me a chance at happiness, and look at the mess I've made of it!* Irritably, she yanked the heavy damask curtains closed and hurried back into the kitchen.

❧

"My, my, my, you all don't know how long it's been since me and my boys had us a real home-cooked meal!" Rochelle Jones exclaimed, her wide, ebony face highlighting the whiteness of her brilliant smile. "Ain't that right, boys?"

Darnell, Darius, and Dasusa Jones, ranging in age from five to seven, bobbed their cropped black heads in unison. Rochelle had come up North looking for work when the factory in her small Southern town closed down, but she had ended up a crack-addict on the streets of Baltimore. She was off drugs now and lived with her children in a homeless shelter. Brenda's church was funding her education at a vocational school. As it turned out, the young single mother had quite a flare for word processing and the makings of a drill sergeant of an office manager.

"We're just so glad you're here." Louise passed Darnell, the oldest of the boys, the platter of carved turkey. "This is what Christmas is all about."

"It certainly is," echoed Marcie, who was busy loading her plate with mashed sweet potatoes topped with roasted, buttered pecans laced with brown sugar. "Brian and Betty are always glad to have kids to play with."

Yeah, especially since Angelo's not here, Brenda thought with a wrench of her heart.

"Mrs. Ford, I ain't never seen such a pretty tablecloth." The black woman fingered the soft, heavy lace.

"Oh, thank you. This lace belonged to my grandmother. She made it herself and brought it with her from South Carolina," Mrs. Ford began as she launched into one of her favorite subjects, the family history.

Brenda realized that, until now, she'd been oblivious to the immense effort her mother had expended on the dinner—a meal for thirteen people, including all four of Marcie's children: her seven-year-old twins, Brian and Betty, ten-year-old Ben, and, of course, Tori. The table was straight out of a Norman Rockwell painting.

The candles cast their flickering gold over the cream tablecloth, the sparkling crystal, the polished silverware, and Louise's best rose-patterned china. The satisfying smell of roast turkey blended with the sage of the dressing and the buttery, yeasty aroma of Marcie's freshly baked rolls. The clink of ice, the crackle of the fire, the soft strains of Michael W. Smith's worshipful Christmas music—all contributed to the poignant scene. With a guilty pang, Brenda realized that, beyond brewing the tea, she hadn't been much help.

"Everything looks great, Mom," she blurted out.

"Thank you, darling."

Even though her mother didn't say anything about the two missing dinner guests, Brenda could see the sympathy in her eyes. Parnell had telephoned her mom just before the family sat down to eat, and had excused himself and Angelo. *He didn't even have the decency to talk to me.* Quickly, Brenda looked away, afraid that, given too much sympathy, she'd break into tears and ruin the meal for everyone.

She was glad that at least the Jones family didn't seem to notice her low spirits. "Now, Mr. Ford, I want you to tell me the honest-to-God truth," began Rochelle. "Am I wastin' my time signing up with those Habitat for Humanity folk? You think me and my kids will ever get us a home of our own?"

Brenda's dad, Dr. Donald Ford, a tall, balding man who ran the

Christ-Centered Counseling Services with his psychologist wife, looked across the table at Rochelle with as much compassion as if she'd been his own daughter. "Hope is one of the greatest virtues, Rochelle, second only to love," he said. "When we hope, we're letting God know we expect Him to answer our prayers."

"How come?" piped up seven-year-old Darnell. "How do we know God's gonna answer our prayers?"

"That's a good question, son, one that folks older than you have asked. Jesus told us that God is like a good Father, and we are His children. If we ask Him for bread, He's not going to give us stones. If we're hungry for a fish sandwich, He's not going to serve up a snake."

"Stones would be pretty hard on your teeth, wouldn't they, Grandpa?" quipped Brian, nudging his twin sister. She responded by pulling a face.

"You bet," replied Dr. Ford, giving his perky grandson a wink. "So, Darnell, because God is like a kind Father, we can count on Him to take care of us and not ignore our prayers."

"Dr. Ford, we don't got no daddy. He went away and he don't give us nothing—not bread, not stones. Nothin'." Darnell eyed his mother, then Dr. Ford. Brenda said a quick prayer that the Holy Spirit would give her father wisdom.

"I'm sorry to hear that, Darnell," he said slowly and deliberately, as if weighing each word before it passed his lips. "I'll bet it's hard for you to see God as a kind Father when your own daddy doesn't take care of you and your momma. I don't think Jesus would mind if you thought of God as being like your momma. Always kind. Always looking after your needs. In fact, Jesus once described himself as a mother hen who wanted to gather all the baby chicks under her wing."

All the children giggled. Brian flapped his arms. Even Brenda couldn't help smiling.

There was a twinkle in her dad's eye as he continued. "If you asked your momma for a slice of bread, do you think she'd give you a piece of rock?"

"No way!" Darnell said with the greatest of emphasis. "My momma loves me!"

"That's right!" Dr. Ford flashed a smile at Rochelle who looked teary-eyed. "Your momma wouldn't want you to break those fine, white teeth. And because your momma loves you, she's only going to give you what's best for you, what you need."

"And I don't need to be eatin' no rocks!" Darnell beamed as he broke into a toothy grin. "None of them snakes, neither."

Dr. Ford smiled at him and returned his attention to Rochelle as he passed her the gravy boat. "So, Rochelle, I think you can live with hope, expecting that the Lord will answer your prayer and provide for your needs, whether it be through fixing up a house with the Habitat for Humanity people or some other way."

"Thank you, Dr. Ford," said Rochelle. "I sure needed to hear that. You're so right, I need to live with hope and not be givin' in to these doubts and discouragements. Givin' in can't be pleasing to the Lord, I reckon."

At least someone is living with hope, Brenda thought glumly as she pushed her sweet potatoes around the plate, hoping no one would notice how little she was actually eating. *I want to live with hope, Lord, and trust You to work Your will in my life and do what's best for me. I'm sorry to be a Doubting Thomas, but I'm finding it really hard to see how the blowup with Parnell isn't a whole bunch of gravel in my teeth. I don't even know if there's any hope left, Lord. And I certainly don't have any joy.*

But Brenda did her best to hide her despondence as the meal progressed toward the dessert and a triumphant-looking Tori emerged from the kitchen carrying two steaming, fragrant pies. "Apple and mincemeat!" she cried. "I used an authentic English recipe I found in a book about Christmas in Charles Dickens's time."

"Bravo, darling." Louise Ford wiped her mouth with her napkin and rose. "I'll get the coffee."

Brenda was silently calculating how long dessert and gift-opening would take so that she could gracefully slip away when the doorbell rang. Her heart lurched. Could it be?

"Brenda, darling, could you get that while I take care of the coffee?" said her mother. "We'll have dessert in the den downstairs. I've rented a copy of "It's a Wonderful Life."

The younger kids didn't need to be asked twice. Like a herd of stampeding cattle, they bounded down the basement steps, singing "Jingle Bells" at the top of their lungs. The older kids and adults followed, humming rather than bellowing. Mrs. Ford began cutting the pies, but Brenda could feel her mother's attention fixed on her as she crossed the black and white tiled floor of the foyer. She hesitated a moment before she turned the brass knob on the massive front door. Quite unexpectedly, she felt a little queasy. *Help me, Lord. If it's Parnell, what am I going to say?*

But she didn't have an opportunity to say a word before Angelo streaked through the door, a blur of red snow coat and black rubber boots, and began pummeling her with his small fists. "You lied to me! You lied!" he cried, tears streaming down his flushed, anguished face. "You promised to be my mother! But you're going to leave me!"

Brenda gazed past the small curly head to Parnell. His tanned face looked eerily pale in the porch light, and she thought she saw a trace of panic in his eyes. "He insisted on coming. . ."

Brenda, glad that the guests were out of earshot in the basement, scooped Angelo up. "We should talk in the library," she explained. "We have. . .guests."

Without a word, Parnell brushed past her, bringing in the chill of the evening with him. She caught sight of her mother, peering down the hallway as Parnell disappeared into the library. Lines of concern furrowed Mrs. Ford's face. "Go on, now," she whispered urgently. "I'll close the front door."

With Angelo clinging to her neck, his legs wrapped around her waist like a vise, Brenda followed Parnell. All the way down the long corridor, she hugged him tight, whispering over and over, "Hush now, sweetheart. Everything's going to be all right."

She hesitated at the entrance to the library.. Parnell stood in the darkened room, his left arm slung on top of the marble mantelpiece, his head resting on his forearm. Balancing Angelo as he sobbed into her neck, Brenda flipped the light switch with her elbow and pushed the heavy door closed with her foot. Gingerly, she lowered herself into a blue velvet wing chair next to the fireplace and tried to soothe the boy.

"Don't cry, honey. Tell me why you think I lied to you."

He wouldn't look at her. The only answer she got was a bout of convulsive sobbing. Angelo clung to her even tighter. Alarmed, she looked over at Parnell.

"I told him why we weren't coming to dinner," he said, never raising his head.

"What exactly did you say to the child?"

"The truth. That our engagement was off."

"Just like that? You broke his heart, just like that?" Concern for her own misery evaporated. She patted Angelo's back. The boy had stopped sobbing and started hiccuping.

"Just what did you expect me to tell him? Should I have tried to hide the truth, or just lied outright?"

"Parnell, why are you so angry?" She studied the big man standing in her father's library. His clothes, his demeanor, his graceful, large frame—all should have put him right at home in a gentleman's room filled with leather and books. But something didn't fit. This wasn't the Parnell she knew. Not this bitter, angry man.

"You could have found a way to break it to him more gently," she replied evenly, biting back the harsh words she itched to say, to trade barb for barb. She quelled her urge to defend herself. *It won't do any good to fly off the handle again. Stay calm. Count to ten. Jesus, make me meek and gentle like You.*

Parnell plunged his hands into the pockets of his tailored overcoat. His black hair and beard looked stark against the light gray wool. "Sometimes it's better to be up front with the truth. At least a clean, honest wound heals quicker."

Brenda looked away, fixing her gaze on the ashes in the grate. Cold, black, charred—as dead as their love. The lump in her throat felt as hard as a lump of coal, and she didn't trust herself to speak. Instead, she rocked Angelo, feeling him relax against her, his small body molding to hers. It broke her heart to know that it was his trust in her that was allowing him to let go his anxiety, to finally drift into an exhausted slumber.

At length, when Angelo was asleep, she stopped rocking. She glanced up to find Parnell watching her. "It's time to leave," he said, walking toward her. He unbuttoned his coat, took Angelo out of her arms, and nestled the sleeping child against his cream cable-knit sweater. Drawing his coat halfway over the boy's body, he looked down at Brenda. "Good-bye," he said, simply, but with a finality that stabbed like steel.

He can't just walk out—not like this! She sat shaken, hands gripping the arms of the chair. Parnell stopped by the carved wooden door, but didn't turn around to face her. For a moment he stood silently, his body rigid, clutching his sleeping son. The only sounds came from the ticking of the clock on the marble mantel.

This was her last chance to make peace.

"Parnell," she began, "I'm sorry for whatever's hurting you, and I apologize for the abominable way I acted last night."

He turned. Some emotion that she couldn't identify flickered across his face before he checked it. "Thank you," he said quietly, the rancor suddenly gone from his voice. "I'm sorry, too, Brenda. But maybe it's better this way. I wish you'd told me the truth. . . I wish they'd told me the truth. Secrets can end up destroying the person they're supposed to protect."

Before she could open her mouth to ask what he meant, Parnell was gone.

For a long time, Brenda sat motionless in the stillness, staring into the ashes, turning Parnell's last words over in her mind. He wished they'd told him the truth. *The truth about what? Who are "they"?*

Who else had hurt Parnell Pierce through silence?

Maybe she wasn't the only one guilty of keeping secrets.

twelve

Thirty minutes later, Brenda sat alone in her mother's kitchen, staring dully at the mound of ice cream atop her spoon and wondering how many millions of calories lurked in one half-gallon tub of Ben and Jerry's double chocolate.

"My darling daughter, isn't that your third bowlful?" Louise Ford suddenly appeared in the doorway, pinning Brenda with her cool blue eyes.

Brenda looked up. "What would you say if I said I'd lost count?"

"Well, I'd say, 'My rates are cheap.'"

"My mother, the counselor! Just what I'd expect from you." Brenda pushed the container across the kitchen island and motioning for her mother to pull up a stool. "Here, help yourself. Better be quick while there's some left."

"Don't mind if I do." Mrs. Ford crossed the slate floor and slid onto the pink leatherette stool. Pinks and mauves echoed around the kitchen decor that rivaled layouts in *House Beautiful*. From the sleek, blond oak cabinets to the hanging brass cookware to the six floor-to-ceiling paneled windows and two French doors overlooking sculptured shrubbery and old English flowerbeds, the room reflected the personality of the mistress of the house—gracious, elegant, and refined.

"Is the movie over?" asked Brenda.

"No, it's barely halfway through." Louise Ford crossed her legs and smoothed the skirt of her yellow knit suit. "Your. . .eh. . . surprise visit might not have taken as much time as you thought."

"You mean it didn't take an eternity?"

"Exactly." Mrs. Ford peered into the almost empty ice cream carton. "Do you know about the chocolate mocha at the back of the freezer?"

"Yep. I was planning on getting to it next."

Her mom hopped down from the stool and walked to the massive built-in freezer that masqueraded as another oak cabinet. "Are we talking death by chocolate, darling?" she asked sweetly as she rummaged at the back of the top shelf where she stashed her one indulgence.

"You've got that right. How did you know?"

"Well, I noticed you're not wearing your engagement ring, for starters. I assume it didn't fall down the drain. Want to talk? A problem shared is a problem halved." She set the fresh Ben and Jerry's in the middle of the island and fetched herself a bowl and spoon.

Brenda briefly wondered how her mother managed to still look polished and glamorous, even at the end of a busy day. She let out a long breath and pushed her bowl away. "Thanks for the chocolate empathy, Mom, but I've had enough sugar. Ice cream isn't gonna fix my problem, I'm afraid."

"What happened?" Mrs. Ford ladled two large spoonfuls—her limit—into a blue cobalt bowl. "Sometimes it helps to just start, anywhere."

"Well, let's put it this way, a sugar high doesn't take away feelings of helplessness."

"Helplessness? Anything to do with Parnell's visit today?"

Brenda noticed that her mother was listening rather than eating. "He came for Angelo's sake, he said. The child was devastated. Accused me of lying. You heard him."

"Yes, I heard. But. . .lying?"

"I promised I'd be his stepmother. Now that the engagement is off, he. . ." Brenda choked up.

"He feels betrayed."

"Yes," she said miserably. "Poor baby. First he loses his mother; then he loses me. I don't know how he's going to handle this one."

"Probably not well."

Brenda let out a sob.

Louise stroked her chin with her thumb and forefinger. After several moments, she asked, "Who broke off the engagement?"

Brenda looked into her mother's china blue eyes. "I did, I suppose. After the service last night, Parnell said he wanted to postpone the wedding. I objected, and he insisted. Well, I guess I overreacted a bit. I got mad and gave him back his ring." Brenda shrugged. "I figured his asking for a postponement was just an excuse—that he'd really changed his mind about getting married. I know you say he's just hiding out in his cave, but it sure feels like he's fallen out of love with me."

"Did he say so?"

"No. As a matter of fact, he denied it."

Mrs. Ford shifted her weight, recrossing her legs. "Have I ever told you the story about the dog I nearly ran over on the highway?"

"No." Brenda wondered what a dog story had to do with Parnell.

"I was on my way home from giving a marriage preparation course. It was just before last Christmas, very dark and very cold. I was driving along I-175 and I noticed cars in front swerving, as if trying to avoid hitting something. Then I saw a big yellow Labrador standing halfway across the right lane. Just standing there! I was going to drive by, but I simply couldn't. I pulled over, got out of my car, and yanked him off the road."

Brenda imagined her mother in heels and cashmere, pulling a reluctant dog off the interstate. "Mom! Isn't it dangerous to stop on the expressway like that? Besides, that dog could have bitten you."

"Yes, I know. But I was very careful, darling. And what else could I have done? The next car could have hit him. But that's not all. After I got him onto the shoulder, I realized he was blind! That poor thing must have been so dazed and confused! Just then, a car pulled up behind me, with a frantic young couple inside. It was their dog. He'd gotten out when visitors arrived for the wife's baby shower. They were both crying and the dog went wild. . .

jumped all over them, licking their faces. . ." Mrs. Ford smiled at the memory.

A pang of pity shot through Brenda's heart. A blind dog on the expressway. Could there be anything more pitiable? "I stand corrected, Mom. You did the right thing. I'm just glad you didn't get hurt. Frightened animals can be vicious."

"Oh, he snapped at first, out of fear probably. But I held him firmly by the back of the collar where he couldn't reach me. And as soon as I got him out of the blare of the traffic, he calmed down and was a real sweetheart. But think about it, Brenda. We're quick to feel pity for a hurting animal or a blind dog, but slow to feel compassion for a hurting human who's built thick walls of defense around himself."

The penny dropped. "Ouch! You're talking about Parnell, aren't you?"

"Bingo! He's snarling because he's hurt. I think whatever's bothering him goes beyond you and Emma. My professional instincts tell me there's something much deeper going on here. If it were just your secret alone, he could deal with it, I'm sure. But whatever his problem is, it's gotten the better of him and he's trapped out on the highway like the blind Lab."

"Oh, Mom, I think you're right! Tonight, in the library, he said something that makes me suspicious."

"Suspicious of what?" Louise narrowed her gaze.

"That I haven't been the only person keeping secrets. . ."

"Very interesting. What exactly did he say?"

"Well, I apologized for flying off the handle, hoping we could patch things up, and he said something about secrets destroying the people they're supposed to protect."

"That's certainly true."

"Then he said he wished I'd told him the truth. . .and he wished they'd told him the truth."

"'They'? Do you have any idea who he was talking about?"

"Not a clue. He left before I could ask. But, Mom, he was so miserable. . .it breaks my heart."

Mrs. Ford circled the rim of her bowl with one tapered finger. "Hmm, curiouser and curiouser. I think our Parnell might just have a few little secrets of his own, and they could be weighing on him heavily."

"I know he feels betrayed. Even from his tone of voice when he said, 'I wish you'd told me.'"

"Well, betrayal is a difficult thing to deal with, of course—and to forgive." Mrs. Ford started nibbling at her ice cream. "No point letting it melt," she said as she savored the chilled creaminess. After a moment, she continued, "I know you've been hurt terribly, darling, and it pains me to see you suffer. But sometimes I find myself agreeing with C.S. Lewis. . ."

"OK, what'd he say this time?" Brenda gave an exaggerated sigh. She liked to tease both her parents about their fondness for the works of the British apologist.

"He said he didn't think God created us to be happy."

"Well, I could certainly agree with that right now."

"Lewis figures God created us to grow up and learn to love. Happiness isn't the most important thing. Love is. God wants us to learn to love Him and each other, and that includes loving Parnell, even at his worst. After all, love that's unwilling to make sacrifices is not love at all."

"I know what you're saying, Mom, but part of me wants to dig in my heels and whine, 'But he hurt my feelings!'"

Mrs. Ford glanced from her empty bowl to the tub of ice cream and almost succumbed to temptation. Instead, she snapped the lid back on the container and returned it to the freezer. "You're strong enough to rise above self-pity, forgive him, and move on to uncovering the real problem. Don't quit now. Fight for your man!"

Brenda chuckled. She liked the sound of that. "Got any ammunition?"

Mrs. Ford walked around to Brenda's side of the island and gave her a hug. "You know this already, Brenda, but it's worth repeating. The popular image of love as a spontaneous, irresistible impulse is a lie, in spite of all the songs and novels to the contrary. Our culture has reduced love to a passing emotion. Real love is about keeping your commitment when the going gets tough. So Parnell's problems are your problems."

Brenda listened attentively, noticing that her earlier sense of helplessness was dissipating. "Go on, Mom. I'm all ears."

"To love is to give ourselves, which, needless to say, doesn't come easily to our fallen nature," Mrs. Ford continued, squeezing Brenda's arm affectionately. "Without the grace of God, it doesn't come at all. Love is a deliberate choice to dedicate ourselves to the well-being of another, whatever the cost. And, darling, it can cost everything."

Brenda nodded. "Scary, but true."

"You bet. That's why our Lord sweated blood. It takes courage to love because we instinctively avoid self-sacrifice."

"To return to your dog metaphor, are you saying what I think you're saying?"

"Try me."

Brenda counted off on her fingers. "First, Parnell is a dog." She giggled. "Second, I'd better take care that he doesn't bite me. Third, it's time to drag him off the freeway."

Her mom gave a wry smile. "Well, that's the general idea, but without the canine connotations. It does seem that Parnell has turned out to be a more complex person than you'd originally thought. Would I be right?"

"Yeah. 'Fraid so."

"So you have two choices. First, you can decide the relationship isn't worth the hassle or the risk. That's what many people do—even after they've said their marriage vows.

"Or, second, you can revise your original assumptions about Parnell—update them, so to speak. So he's got some deep issues, perhaps some secrets, just like you had. If you want to save the relationship, you've got to let go of your illusions and your disappointment and accept the person Parnell really is."

Brenda nodded. "That makes sense. But, Mom, I've said some awful things. Do you really think there's still hope for Parnell and me?"

"Where there's life, there's hope, Brenda, darling. I've seen too many relationships restored to doubt that. If God raised Jesus from the dead, He can raise your relationship. . .if you want Him to."

Brenda sighed. "You're right, Mom. As a Christian, I can't just give up on Parnell. But it's not going to be easy."

"I know. We don't wrestle against flesh and blood, as the Bible warns us, so it's not Parnell you're fighting, darling. Satan is our real enemy. By the way, how's your prayer life?"

"Well, I pray and meditate on the Word for an hour before I go to work."

"Good girl, but now that you're in the heat of battle, you need to step up your attack. I'd recommend you get up earlier each day and pray an extra thirty minutes for Parnell. Ultimately, only God can heal and change him, but remember, you're a prayer warrior, fighting for the man you love."

❧

As Brenda drove away from her parents' home, she felt hopeful, even lighthearted. Her mother certainly had a gift for cutting through the fog and getting to the heart of the matter. Her message wasn't a spineless platitude, either; it was a challenge, a spiritual battle cry, "Fight for your relationship! Don't let the enemy tear you apart!"

As Brenda followed a snow plow down Little Patuxent Parkway, she resolved that she wouldn't give up fighting for Parnell. The real battle was in the heavenly realm. "Deliver him, Lord, from whatever's oppressing him, weighing him down, pulling him away from me," she prayed aloud as she carefully maneuvered the icy street. Her mind drifted to Rita Andreas, her assistant. "And, Lord, protect Rita. Give her strength to resist temptation. . ."

She wondered how Rita was doing. With all the romance surrounding the Christmas season, what if Reggie's demands had gotten out of hand? Suddenly, Brenda felt a strong, unexpected urge to offer Rita some encouragement in her battle for chastity. Taking this urge as the prompting of the Holy Spirit, she turned her car around in one of Columbia's many cul-de-sacs and headed back downtown toward Rita's small apartment.

When she pulled into Pierce Estates, Brenda noticed that Rita's place was dark. *She must be out with Reggie. I should have called first.* Nevertheless, she pulled into a parking space, killed the engine, and walked up the flight of stone steps to Rita's second-floor apartment. She checked her watch. Nine o'clock. A little late for a social call, but this was the holiday season. Anyway, she was here now, and it was too cold to stand outside shivering. She pulled the neck of her coat closed and pushed the doorbell.

No answer. Brenda rang again, two short staccato jabs with her index finger. She was just about the leave when she heard a noise inside. The dead bolt was pulled back. The door opened.

Brenda gasped. In the light from the street lamps, Rita looked haggard and ill. Her face was swollen and blotchy from crying. Her makeup had run, leaving black smudges on her cheeks. Her long, black hair was tossed and wild, as if she'd been pulling at it. Her dark eyes focused on Brenda.

"Rita! What's the matter?"

The young woman burst into tears. She moved her lips, but no words came out.

"I'm coming in, OK?" Brenda said softly, putting her hand on the doorknob.

Rita nodded and stepped back, allowing Brenda to walk into the efficiency apartment. In the dim light flooding in from the parking lot, the first thing Brenda noticed was the untouched Christmas dinner on the table. She turned on the metal 1950s style floor lamp and illuminated the sad scene. Apparently, Rita had gone to a lot of trouble to prepare a traditional dinner. Her dinette table was set for two, with plastic placements showing Santa and his reindeer. The turkey—the size of a large chicken—sat, roasted and stuffed. . .and uneaten. The mashed potatoes looked cold and unappetizing. The green peas, dried and shriveled.

Watching Brenda survey the scene, Rita let out a wail, covered her face with her hands, and bolted into the living room area behind the kitchen. Brenda closed the front door, ran after Rita, and found her friend crumpled on the floor beside the old, tattered couch, sobbing into the cushions. Gingerly, she knelt down beside her.

"Rita, something awful has happened to you. But nothing is so bad that God can't help."

"Y—you're. . .wrong," she sobbed. "You don't know. . ."

"You know my story, Rita," Brenda said, laying her hand on Rita's heaving shoulder. "You read in the paper about the stupid mistakes I made. If God helped me, He can help you."

Rita's sobs subsided, and she sat, her head buried in her hands. Finally, she raised her head and, eyes wide, looked at Brenda. "Maybe. . .yes, I guess you do know. You've been there."

Brenda's stomach lurched. She knew what was coming, but she asked anyway, hoping against hope it wasn't so. "What is it, Rita?"

"Brenda. . .I'm pregnant."

"Oh, Rita!" Brenda's voice caught on the tears rising in the back of her throat. For a moment, time stood still.

The light from the kitchen seeped into the darkened living room, casting shadows on Rita's tear-stained face. Her lips were swollen. Her mysterious, dark, Cherokee eyes fastened on Brenda. She didn't look away, didn't look down, didn't blink. Slowly, she lifted a brow, daring Brenda to say something.

Oh, Holy Spirit, please give me the right words. Brenda glanced around the darkened room with its white plastic coffee table, small imitation Christmas tree, and flickering black and white TV with the sound turned down. *This lamb of Yours is hurting, Lord. Use me as Your instrument to help her.*

"Rita, I'm sorry, so sorry. Did you tell Reggie?"

The young woman started sobbing again, this time in noisy, gulping breaths. Without being told, Brenda guessed what had happened.

"You told him tonight, didn't you?" Brenda began, her voice soft. She wanted to make it as easy as possible for Rita to confide in her. "You fixed him a nice dinner and then you broke the news, fully expecting him to propose right on the spot. Isn't that how it happened? Only he didn't propose. He walked out."

Rita looked up in surprise. She pushed back her jet black hair. "How did you know?"

"Just like you said, I've been there. I did exactly the same thing. I thought Brad would be so happy about the baby, he'd marry me in a heartbeat. He always said marriage was just a piece of legal paper. . .loving one another was what counted. . ."

Rita covered her face with her hands. "Just like. . .R-Reggie. J-just like h-him. H-he says if I love him, I won't ruin his music career. That was the last thing he said before he left. That's why he wants me to. . ." She broke off, her voice fading into a faint squeak.

Brenda didn't need to be told Reggie's demand, either. She finished Rita's sentence for her: "He wants you to. . .have an abortion."

Startled, Rita glanced up. "How. . .?"

Brenda scooted over beside her friend and slipped her arm around the shaking woman's shoulders. "I know. . .because Brad wanted me to 'get rid of the problem,' too."

Rita leaned against Brenda. "Reggie said we'd get married. . . later," she whispered. "He said this wasn't a good time in his career, that a shotgun wedding would be bad for his public image . . . He said we could have other children. . .later."

Brenda hugged Rita tighter. Silently, she prayed for God to

strengthen Rita's courage so the young woman could look the truth in the face and be set free. "He's lying, Rita. He hasn't kept his promises—to you or to God. He's even misrepresenting himself to his fans. They think he's something he's not."

"I know, I know. And it makes me feel like such a fool. As the saying goes, 'Why buy the cow when you can get the milk for free?'" Rita's voice was edged with bitterness.

"I know what it feels like to be used, Rita. It's devastating. But in God's eyes, you're not an object to be thrown aside. Look at the woman caught in adultery in the Gospel of John. She was scorned in society's eyes, even condemned to death by stoning. But remember how Jesus treated her?"

Rita squirmed uncomfortably. Her face flushed. "Uh. . .I don't quite remember that story. . ."

"The Pharisees and teachers of the law flung the poor woman—not the man, mind you—at Jesus' feet. She was frightened out of her wits. Jesus said to the crowd, 'He that is without sin cast the first stone.' One by one, the crowd melted away, convicted by their own consciences. Finally, only Jesus and the woman were left. He gently told her He did not condemn her, and that she should go and sin no more."

"Oh, Brenda. . .that's beautiful. Do you really think He'd do the same for me?"

Brenda grinned. "I don't just think so; I know so. He did it for me. Hitting rock bottom was a blessing in disguise. It forced me to turn to the Lord."

A smile softened the angular planes of Rita's face. "I'm just like that woman. I've been dodging the truth, I guess. Reggie wasn't. . .the first. . ."

"Well, facing the truth is half the battle," Brenda said. "My mother told me that tonight. By the way, where's your mother? I thought she lived with you."

Under her green and brown tartan shirt, Rita shrugged her slim shoulders. "Oh, Mom. She doesn't live here anymore. She moved in with her new boyfriend last month."

"Oh." A pang of pity shot through Brenda. Rita's mother, a teacher's aid at the local high school, had gone through a string of boyfriends since her second divorce. *Rita certainly hasn't had much in the way of a godly example, Lord. I wonder how well I would have done without Mom's guidance.* Brenda remembered that day in her pharmacy when she'd felt the urge to confide her whole story to Rita, but hadn't followed through. Now she shook her head at her own lack of compassion.

Brenda took a deep breath. "Your Mom's. . .choices. . .have been hard on you, haven't they?"

Rita's eyes misted over. "Yes, they have, but I'd never tell her that. Mom insists she's not doing anything wrong, that she and Fred are adults and it's nobody's business what they do in private. They're not going to have children, she says, so why should they get married? She's even going to a new church where they turn a blind eye to couples living together."

Brenda stared at the edge of the worn orange throw covering the couch. "It's hard to do the right thing when people around you aren't," she said. "That's why it's a mistake for your Mom to say it's nobody's business. Her lifestyle has affected you, for one."

Brenda drew her legs close to her body, glad that she'd worn her heavy corduroy pants and oversize woolen sweater. She sighed, then continued. "We're truly living in the midst of a 'crooked, perverse generation,' Rita, just like the Bible says. Even some churches are compromising God's truth. We've got to be strong, try to be good examples."

"Huh! I haven't been much of an example," said Rita, laying her hand on her still-flat abdomen. "And in a few months, I'll be an even worse one."

"Don't be so hard on yourself. You'll be a witness to the sanctity of life, even a life that comes at an inconvenient time. When you're doing the right thing, it really doesn't matter what other people think. God's opinion is the only one that counts in the end. What's important is, are you ready to ask God's forgiveness? Are you truly sorry for your mistakes?"

Rita shuddered a little. "I think so. It's taken my life falling in pieces around my feet, but I think I'm ready. I know I need to repent, to change. Thank God He's been so patient with me."

Brenda squeezed her friend's hand. "Let's ask Him to forgive you and give you another chance," she offered. "And remember, secondary virginity isn't just a pious-sounding phrase. When we're truly sorry, God wants to give you a clean slate."

"Will He really do that? I mean, will He let me start over? It sounds too easy."

"I know it sounds too good to be true. But the Bible says that 'if we confess our sins, God will forgive our sins' and make us white as snow—as if those things never really happened! That's why Christ died—to pay for what we have done."

"Incredible!" Rita breathed, smiling through a sheen of tears. "Will you pray for me, Brenda?"

Both women closed their eyes and lifted their hearts to their heavenly Father. They sat on the floor of the dimly lit apartment, unaware of the angels rejoicing over the repentance of one sinner.

thirteen

Brenda sliced into the small turkey, shaving off three slices of breast meat. "You sit, Rita. I'll warm up a plate for you."

"OK, boss. If you insist." Rita flopped down onto one of her turquoise plastic kitchen chairs. In the harsh, overhead light, she looked disheveled and exhausted. "To tell you the truth, I'm pooped."

"I can tell." Brenda spooned mashed potatos onto the plate. She almost decided against the wrinkled peas, but opted to try a few. Maybe they'd reconstitute in the microwave if she smothered them with gravy. "We need to feed you. After all, you're eating for two."

Rita looked a little dumbfounded. She ran her hand through her waist-length black hair. "Yeah. . .I guess. I just hadn't thought of being pregnant as. . .well, you know, really carrying a baby. I have a hard time imagining a real live person. Know what I mean?"

Brenda chuckled as the pressed the buttons on the microwave. "I know exactly what you mean. It takes a while for the reality to sink in that there's a little person growing inside you. But even the word fetus is Latin for 'unborn baby.' Believe me, Rita, there's a little girl or boy growing inside your body right now."

"A little boy or girl?" A smile began forming at the corners of Rita's mouth.

"Yep. Can you imagine? Your baby's sex is already set."

"Amazing. Totally awesome."

The microwave bell dinged and Brenda retrieved the steaming plate and placed it in front of Rita. "Mustard? Ketchup?"

"No, thanks. But maybe a little iced tea. Or wait, I think there's still a can of cranberry juice in the refrigerator."

"You eat. I'll fetch. You need to relax. You've had an emotionally draining day."

Rita flashed a grateful smile that warmed Brenda's heart. How well she remembered the lonely, weary days of her own pregnancy when she would have cried with joy for a helping hand or a kind word. She popped the lid of the juice can and poured the sparkling liquid into a tall glass and plopped in a couple of ice cubes, glad that she could bring a little comfort to Rita.

"Aren't you having anything to eat yourself?" Rita asked.

"No, I'm stuffed. My mother's good cooking, you know. Well, actually, now that we're telling the truth and shaming the devil, that's not quite correct. I hardly ate any dinner, but I did scarf down three bowls of chocolate ice cream afterwards."

Rita giggled. "Why?"

"Oh, I was upset."

"Your turn. Tell me about it," Rita said as she bit into a piece of turkey.

Putting the events of the last twenty-four hours into words helped Brenda order them in her mind. Rita listened as she ate, occasionally indicating shock, surprise, or dismay. When Brenda recounted the events following the Christmas Eve service, Rita shook her head. "You mean, the engagement's off?"

"Yeah. But not for long. Not if I have anything to do with it."

"Brenda! How can you be so confident?"

"Well, the story doesn't end there. After the ice-cream bonanza, my mother and I had a heart-to-heart in the kitchen. We figured out from things Parnell said that there's more bothering him than just my revelation."

"What could it be?"

"I don't know. . .yet. Seems I'm not the only one who's kept secrets from him, though."

"Ooh! I love a mystery!"

"I've no idea what was kept from him, or by whom. But Mom reminded me that if I really love Parnell, I won't give up on him. If he's got a problem, it's my problem, too."

Rita played with her fork, scooting the last few peas around her plate. "How I wish Reggie would think like that. But as far as he's concerned, this baby's my problem—and mine alone."

"I know how much that hurts, Rita. But I want you to know, even though Reggie's not with you, I am. My family is, too. You're not facing this alone."

Tears spilled down Rita's face. She grabbed a napkin and mopped her face, her shoulders heaving. Brenda hurried around the table and stood behind her friend, placing one hand on each shoulder, praying for God to surround Rita with the comfort of His presence.

"How am I going to manage, Brenda? Since Mom left, I've barely been able to pay my rent. What happens if I can't work? I've heard horror stories about nausea and swollen legs and. . ." She broke into a fresh torrent of tears.

"That's fear talking, Rita. Those things might happen, but they might not. Some women sail through pregnancy with barely a complaint." Brenda dropped down on her knees and took Rita's damp face between her hands. "Now, you listen to me, sister, I'm not deserting you. You've got a job. If you can't work, I'll hire a replacement until you can. If you can't pay your rent, you can live in my spare room. We can work this out, do you hear? You're not alone. We're family, God's family."

Rita relaxed visibly, as if an iron weight had just dropped from her shoulders. "How can I thank you?" she rasped.

"By taking good care of yourself and that baby."

"I will," she promised, looking Brenda in the eye. "But I want to do something else, something to help you as a friend."

Brenda flashed back on her conversation with her mother. "Well, there is something you can do, something very important. . ."

"What is it? I'll do anything."

"Be my prayer partner. . .I need you to fast and pray with me for Parnell and for our relationship to be healed. Can you do that?"

Rita blinked. "Of course. I haven't done much praying recently, but that's going to change. But, Brenda, I'm not so sure about the fasting. . .in my condition, and all."

Brenda laughed. "Silly of me. Of course you can't fast from

food, but you could do another type of fast."

"Such as?"

"Such as giving up something you like—some junk food that's not good for you anyway. What would be a sacrifice for you to forego?"

Rita thought for a moment. "Potato chips. Chocolate."

"Perfect. They're fatty, salty, sugary, and have little nutrition, so it's not going to hurt the baby to give them up. Anything else?"

"Well, how about racy romance novels? I must read six a week. Reading stories about passionate sex before marriage certainly hasn't done me any good. In fact, it's pretty trashy stuff."

"What about some good Christian fiction instead?"

"I'd never even thought of it." Rita clasped Brenda's hands and fell silent for a moment, chewing on her bottom lip. "Brenda, about Parnell and his mysterious problem. . .how much do you really know about him?"

Brenda felt a little defensive, and that bothered her. "What do you mean? I met him a year ago, when I opened the pharmacy. He's my landlord. We go to the same church. We've been engaged for three months."

"But what about his family?" probed Rita, inclining her head to one side and opening her dark eyes wide. "How much do you know about his background?"

"Well, his parents were killed in the same car crash that killed his wife."

"That's just what I mean."

"But Parnell doesn't have any family left except a senile grandma who's in a nursing home in Pennsylvania." Brenda frowned.

"Look, I don't mean to be disrespectful, but you could learn something from Randy O'Reilly's technique. Now, don't look at me like an angry bear, Brenda. What did O'Reilly do when he wanted to find out more about you?"

"He dug around in my past."

"Right. Now, think about it, how much do you really know

about Parnell's past?" Rita arched one black brow.

Brenda hauled in a sharp breath and thought about what Rita had just said. She didn't like the implications, but somehow, the observation had a ring of truth to it. Slowly, she began to put her troubling thoughts into words. "I don't know much about him, not really. Not much beyond where he went to high school and that his father was a minister and that he was an only child."

"So maybe his past is the place to start."

"The only family left is Grandma Prudence, who's nearly a hundred years old and lives in a nursing home. She has Alzheimer's and can't even recognize Parnell or Angelo. It's so painful for Parnell, he only visits her once or twice a year. He used to go every month."

Rita grinned. "Hey, haven't you just spent the last two hours convincing me that nothing is impossible with God on our side?"

Brenda winced. "You learn fast. But asking a woman with no memory to remember—now that's what I'd call a mission impossible."

&

The day after Christmas was a cold, clear Saturday. No more snow fell. But a frigid wind howled across the near-empty parking lot at Thunder Hill Medical Center. The snow plows had packed yesterday's snow into man-sized banks around the edge of the lot, partially obscuring the tall spruces that separated the medical center from the hospital.

Only a few professional offices were open. Brenda had given both Rita and Tori the day off and opened the shop only in the morning, mostly to service the patients in the hospital, whose medical needs knew no vacations. She stood behind the white counter in the pharmacy, counting out a course of a new, stronger antibiotic for an elderly woman suffering from pneumonia, then paused to watch the changing light outside the glass wall facing the parking lot.

The steely sky, heavy with unspent snow, spread its sharp, harsh light over the city. A sudden gust of wind blew a whole flock of sparrows sailing across the parking lot in a squiggly line. In the distance, the sharp, angular shapes of tall high-rises and towering office buildings pierced the skyline. Bright, cold whiteness washed everything in an incandescent light, making the dark buildings stand out in bold relief.

Parnell owned several of those buildings, she knew. He'd built some of the others. He knew every building in this town. He knew every community leader, every builder and contractor, the head of every social service agency. Most people, other than Randy O'Reilly, took pride in knowing Parnell Pierce. When Serena was alive, the Pierces' annual Christmas party was one of the social highlights of the season.

Yet. . .could Rita be right? Could there be a Parnell Pierce neither she nor anyone else knew? A man of secrets, who kept secrets—or from whom secrets had been kept?

Secrets can end up destroying the person they're supposed to protect.

Who was Parnell Pierce, really?

Brenda snapped the lid on the plastic bottle and punched the prescription number into the computer. Her stomach growled. She'd been fasting on a couple of plain crackers and water all day. Now, in the early afternoon, her stomach was registering its protest. She felt a little weak, but steeled her will to see the fast through to the end of the day. From her spiritual reading over the years, Brenda knew that fasting lent an urgency to prayer, and she wanted heaven to know she was committed to her prayers for Parnell.

This was war, and she wasn't going to fight halfheartedly.

Still, images of food kept creeping into her mind. Steaming, fragrant pizza. Sizzling French fries, drizzled in salt, plunged into ketchup. Hot cinnamon rolls, dripping melting vanilla icing. Robust Java coffee, laced with cream. . .

No! she told herself sharply. *Stick to your guns. This is war!*

After filling six prescriptions for hospital patients, including one cancer patient who probably wouldn't live through the night but desperately needed to be relieved of his pain, Brenda tucked her bottles into a sturdy brown paper bag. She'd drop the medicine by the hospital on her way to the car. Without removing her white pharmacy uniform, she slipped into her black wool coat and flipped over the "Closed" sign hanging on the back of the glass door.

She'd just stepped into the cavernous marble lobby and locked the door to her shop when she noticed Parnell's car pull up. Through the main glass doors, she watched him maneuver effortlessly into his assigned spot, unfold his long body from the gleaming green Jaguar, and stride toward the building. *So, he's begun parking in the front lot again.* Her adrenaline pumped, and her mind raced back to the last time she'd seen him, glaring at her angrily in her father's library.

I'm sorry, Brenda. But maybe it's better this way...

Is that right, Parnell Pierce? Well, we'll just see about that!

She melted into the shadows by the staircase. She didn't want him to see her until the last moment. He'd just pocketed his black leather gloves and put his hand on the steel railings, when she stepped out.

His jaw dropped, and he stood, frozen as the marble surrounding him, a granite outcropping set in a building of stone.

The sight of him pulled her up sharp. "Hello, Parnell."

His eyes narrowed and he stared at her without saying a word. She felt she was engaged in a battle of wills, and the first one to speak lost. He said nothing.

Neither did she.

Why did he have to look so good, even now? Tall and darkly handsome like a mysterious stranger in a Western movie, Parnell stood at the bottom of the wide staircase with a careless, powerful air of authority. His face was as bleak and steely as the winter sky Brenda had been watching. Even though he didn't smile or invite her to touch him in any way, she longed to reach out and run her hand through his black, wavy hair and trace one finger across his raven beard, to melt the ice he'd packed around his heart.

She decided to take a stab at that ice, but not before digging her hands deep into her coat pockets so she wouldn't touch him. "Parnell, we've got to talk."

"There's nothing to talk about, Brenda. Not right now."

Lifting her chin, Brenda looked him steadily in the eye,

refusing to break eye contact. "Who else hurt you by their silence?" she asked quietly.

Her words might have been karate chops delivered to his abdomen. She watched him catch him breath and struggle to maintain his composure. *He's a complex man,* she'd heard her mother say, *more complicated than you originally supposed.* Brenda narrowed her eyes. *All right, then, be complicated and complex! But you're not driving me away, mister!*

"Brenda, I don't want to talk about this," he said through clenched teeth. She noted a flash of anger cross his features before he turned his face away.

But she wasn't about to back off. "You're mine, Parnell," she heard herself say, her voice surprisingly calm considering how wildly her heart was thumping. "And I'm yours. We belong together. I'm not going to let you drive me away. I love you too much."

She glanced down at his hand, clenched around the steel railing so tightly that his knuckles had turned white. So, he was angry. Why? At whom?

Suddenly, Parnell looked at her. Brenda's breath caught in her throat at the wretchedness on his face. Torment filled his eyes. His mouth was a twisted line. The sight of his distress startled her so, she staggered slightly. She grasped the railing for balance, grazing his hand as she did so.

Parnell jerked his hand away and, without looking back, loped up the stairs. He took the steps two and three at a time, as if he couldn't get away fast enough.

"I'm not giving up on us!" she shouted after him. "Not now! Not ever!"

Her only reply was the echo of her own voice ringing through the huge, empty stairwell.

&

"Impossible man!" Brenda muttered to herself as she steered her car onto 80 East heading toward Pennsylvania. Why can't he just tell me what's wrong, instead of making me go to the ends of the earth, or to Pennsylvania at least, to try to find out?

She stepped on the gas and blended into the traffic. *Maybe he can't tell you.*

That was a sobering insight. Brenda thought back to the time she couldn't tell Parnell what was troubling her. She simply couldn't bring herself to spit out the words. Fear had struck her dumb. It was like being a prisoner inside her own body, wanting to talk but unable to.

Or like a blind dog on the expressway.

Brenda had never met Granny Prudence Pierce, but she knew the nursing home the old lady lived in was in Danville, Pennsylvania. And now Brenda was running to the matriarch for clues about what was bothering a grandson the woman didn't even recognize anymore! Brenda shook her head as she maneuvered off the highway somewhere in the middle of Pennsylvania to fill up with gas. She was tempted to grab a sandwich at the McDonald's drive-through window, but reminded herself firmly that she was still fasting.

Yes, Granny Pru was a long shot, not to mention a long way from home—both geographically and mentally. Brenda clutched her coat against the biting wind while pumping gas with her free hand. *Yes, but, God specializes in the impossible.* The afternoon was freezing cold, but at least the roads were clear. The gas fumes snaked upward and the smell made her stomach queasy. She had a few saltines in her purse and she'd remembered to bring along a bottle of water. Her stomach would have to be content with that.

She thought about the time Gil Montgomery had set up Parnell and made it look like he was harassing her, defacing the front of her shop with hate graffiti and tormenting her with menacing phone calls. When Brenda had suspected Parnell, he'd stuck by her faithfully, even when she'd told him to go take a hike.

Now the shoe was on the other foot, and, boy, did that shoe pinch!

Granny Pru might be a long shot, she told herself as she slid her credit card through the automated gas teller. But sometimes love demanded a long shot, sometimes a shot in the dark. Brenda just hoped that she wasn't about to shoot herself in the foot.

Or in the heart.

fourteen

The first thing Brenda always noticed about nursing homes was the smell of disinfectant. The Holy Cross Home was no exception. Nevertheless, the facility, nestled at the edge of the huge Geisinger Hospital complex, was bright and cheery. The young nurse on duty, Miss Gertrude Massey, seemed surprised that Prudence Pierce had a visitor, but when Brenda showed identification and explained her relationship to the family, the white-capped nurse cheerfully led the way down the labyrinth of brightly polished corridors.

"Mrs. Pierce is a sweetheart," Nurse Massey chatted as she walked briskly, her crepe soles squeaking against the floor. "You couldn't ask for a nicer patient. I've been here a year now, and I've never heard a complaint from her. That's saying plenty! So many folks aren't happy unless they're complaining! Too bad her mind's going, poor dear. She just sits and stares out the window all day and I find myself wondering where she's wandered off to, if you know what I mean."

Brenda hurried to keep up with Nurse Massey's efficient pace. "I'm afraid I do," she replied. "I see many sad cases in my line of work."

"Oh? Are you a doctor? I noticed your white coat."

Brenda glanced down at her white pharmacy coat peeping out from beneath her open overcoat. "No, I'm a pharmacist, actually."

Nurse Massey looked a little envious. "What I wouldn't have given to go into pharmacy. But my high school grades weren't good enough. Well, here we are. Now, I must warn you, don't be alarmed at her appearance. She's lost weight recently. And, only the Lord knows who she'll think you are."

143

The nurse opened the door to Room 1102 and ushered Brenda in.

It was a pleasant room, with floral patterned wallpaper and a small pink couch and loveseat grouping by the large window. Brenda noted the set of matching pastel prints on the wall, the type found in hotels, and a wooden fireplace with an electric heater in the grate. The room had a homey feel. But there didn't seem to be anyone at home within the woman who sat propped up in bed, her long, thin white hair blending with the white of her cotton nightdress. Granny Pru stared blankly out the window at the late afternoon sky.

"Mrs. Pierce! You've got a visitor, dear," Nurse Massey chirped.

The thin, elderly lady made no indication she heard anything. She continued staring, her hands folded one over the other resting on the turned-down sheet.

"I've got to be getting back to my station," the nurse said to Brenda. "Will you be able to manage by yourself?"

"Yes, thank you."

"If she doesn't respond, try reading some Scripture passages. I think she likes that. Sometimes, if she's agitated, it seems to calm her down," Nurse Massey said, motioning to an open Bible on the coffee table by the window. "I'm a believer myself and I don't think we should ever underestimate the power of the Word of God."

"I'm a Christian, too, Miss Massey."

"I had a feeling you were." The nurse winked and disappeared back down the long corridor, leaving Brenda with the silent stranger.

Lord, I'm here. Now what?

❧

Brenda pulled up a straight-backed wooden chair and sat down beside Mrs. Pierce's hospital-style bed. She cleared her throat, but the old lady didn't acknowledge Brenda's presence. Granny Pru didn't look bad for a woman her age. *But she can't weigh more than ninety pounds,* thought Brenda as she surveyed the frail woman, maybe only eighty-five.

Prudence Pierce's long, narrow face was scored with deep wrinkles. Her razor-sharp nose gave her an elfish look. Her green eyes, pale and vacant, stared into space. Her skin, as translucent as parchment, revealed bluish veins that stood out like tree roots on her gnarled hands.

Brenda noticed the fresh red roses on the old woman's nightstand. Their fragrance waged a losing battle against the sharp, pervasive antiseptic odor. She picked up a small card jammed halfway under the blue ceramic vase. "From Parnell, with love always," it read.

I might have known. Briefly, Brenda wondered how often Parnell sent his grandmother flowers. He probably had a standing order with a nearby florist to send them every week.

Parnell Pierce was like that.

"Mrs. Pierce? Prudence? Granny Pru?" Brenda tried to get the old woman's attention, without success. "My name is Brenda Rafferty. I am. . .or was. . .engaged to your grandson, Parnell. The one who sent the roses."

No answer. The old lady coughed and closed her eyes.

Oh, Lord! Don't tell me I'm on a wild goose chase.

Brenda reached across the bed covers and touched Mrs. Pierce's hand. It felt cold. "Granny Pru, I've come a long way to see you. I'd like to talk with you. . .about your grandson."

No reply.

Brenda couldn't mask the anxiety in her voice. "Granny Pru, I'm in an awful state. Something's terribly wrong with Parnell, but he won't tell me, and I was hoping you'd be able to give me some clue. . .tell me something. . ."

The old lady's eyelids fluttered. She opened her eyes, glancing briefly at Brenda without registering any recognition. Then she turned her attention back to the window. Night was falling fast.

Brenda remembered Nurse Massey's suggestion about reading the Scriptures. Jumping to her feet, Brenda hurried across the room and snatched up the open Bible from atop the oak coffee table. It was opened to the Psalms. Briefly, Brenda wondered if Nurse Massey read through the Psalms systematically for the old lady. She hoped that was the case.

"The nurse told me you liked to hear the Bible," Brenda said as she took her seat again, reaching over to turn on the bedside lamp. A fragile golden glow encircled them, leaving the rest of the room in darkness. Brenda cleared her throat. "If you like, I'll take up where Nurse Massey left off, is that all right?"

The old lady blinked. Brenda wasn't sure if she was trying to communicate, but she took it as a go-ahead and began reading from Psalm 34. "I sought the Lord, and he answered me, and delivered me from all my fears. Look to him and be radiant; so your faces shall never be ashamed. This poor man cried, and the Lord heard him and saved him out of all his troubles. The angel of the Lord encamps around those who fear him, and delivers them. . . ."

Brenda read through that psalm, then the next, and the next. The ancient writings spoke of praise and deliverance, troubles and hope. She drew strength from the words, as countless believers had done before her. Yes, God would deliver her from her troubles, in His time, in His way. Everything was under control. His control. In the meantime, Brenda would trust.

She read for over an hour, but the old lady never stirred. After a long while, Brenda closed the Bible in her lap and sat, hands clasped, watching the darkness enshroud the room and listening to the old lady's steady breathing. She was glad she finally had gotten to meet Parnell's grandmother, if you could call this encounter "meeting" a person, but Brenda also had a sinking feeling in her stomach that she was no nearer her goal of winning back Parnell than when she'd left Columbia that afternoon.

At 6:30, another nurse bustled in. Mrs. Carol Reeves was short, rotund, and middle-aged. "Ah, Mrs. Rafferty, Nurse Massey told me you were still in here. How's Mrs. Pierce? Has she spoken at all?" She switched on the overhead light and drew the curtains across the black panes.

"Not a word."

"Heartbreaking, isn't it? It's no wonder her grandson doesn't visit much anymore. He's a good soul, though. Sends her roses every week."

Yeah. He used to send me roses, too.

"Thank you for taking such good care of Mrs. Pierce," said Brenda, rising to put on her coat. "She's fortunate to have good caretakers."

"We do our best. It's a shame, though, the way a mind goes

sometimes, but the body is still with us. But, really, who knows what she's conscious of? Maybe she knows more than we think. Life is a mystery best left in God's hands, I always say."

Brenda buttoned her coat and walked over to the old lady's bedside. She touched the gnarled hand. "Good-bye, Granny Pru. I wish I'd gotten to know you sooner. I've heard what a sharp cookie you were back then. May the Lord watch over you."

❧

Brenda trudged down the long narrow corridor, her heart heavy. The sight of the old lady, motionless but alive, was distressing. She had more sympathy for Parnell and his reluctance to see his own grandmother in this state. But had she wasted her time, driving across state, just to meet with a woman who in all probability didn't even know she'd had a visitor?

Brenda stopped in front of the glass doors leading to the parking lot and pulled her hooded white cashmere scarf over her head. She was hungry, tired, and wasn't looking forward to the long drive home.

She noticed a small blue Saturn pull up in front of the nursing home. A woman in a bulky coat got out and ran toward the entrance.

"Mrs. Rafferty! Oh, thank goodness you're still here!" Nurse Gertrude Massey barreled through the glass doors.

"Well, hello. I didn't expect to see you again. I thought you must have gone off duty."

Nurse Massey paused to catch her breath and yanked off her woolen hat. Her brown hair was tied back in a sensible bun. "I had, actually. I'd gone a mile down the road, but I couldn't shake the feeling that I should come back to talk to you."

"Me? Why?"

"Here, let's sit and I'll tell you everything I know." The young nurse, still wearing her lilac quilted coat, led the way to a grouping of burgundy easy chairs in the lobby.

"What's all this about?" Brenda sat on the edge of her seat, clutching her purse in her lap.

"I don't rightly know myself, but I just couldn't get it out of my mind that you should know what I saw and heard. . .you know when you get a feeling you should do something and it just won't go away?"

Brenda nodded. "Yes, I know the feeling. But, go on, what did you see?"

The nurse took a deep breath. "It was Mr. Pierce, Parnell Pierce. He came to see Mrs. Pierce just a few weeks ago. That in itself was unusual because he hasn't visited in a long time. And he was very agitated. He was waving a document at Mrs. Pierce. He kept asking, 'Did you know about this? Were you in on this?' He's usually so mild-mannered, it was very much out of the ordinary to see him so upset."

Brenda's pulse quickened. "What was the document?"

"A birth certificate, would you believe? I was afraid he'd upset Mrs. Pierce, so I made him sit down on the couch and brought him a cup of tea. I looked at the document and asked what it had to do with his grandmother."

"Did he say?"

"I tell you, Mrs. Rafferty, the man was shaken. He said he'd just learned he'd been adopted. . .which was bad enough, seeing his parents kept it a secret his whole life. But then he discovered that his birth certificate had been altered to hide the adoption!"

Brenda gasped. "My goodness! Is that legal?"

"Yes, in Maryland, anyway. I can't blame him for being distraught. I'd feel the same way. He apologized for making a scene, but explained that he was so desperate, he hoped maybe Mrs. Pierce might remember something if he showed her the certificate."

"Oh, poor Parnell!"

"I'll say. Must have been quite a shock."

From the dates Nurse Massey gave, Brenda figured out that Parnell's visit had occurred two days after the O'Reilly fiasco outside the courthouse.

Two days after.

But what had happened?

fifteen

It was ten o'clock when Brenda finally got back to Columbia. She walked into her living room exhausted, dazed, and a little weak from hunger. She hung her coat on the coat tree and sank down into her soft chintz couch, still feeling chilled at the remembrance of the events that had transpired at the nursing home.

Brenda reached for her Bible, held it in her lap, and ran her fingers across its smooth leather cover. She turned off the brass lamp beside her on the end table. She was too tired to read, content to hold God's Word in her hands. She breathed deeply and tried to pray, offering her anxieties to God, committing herself to His care.

"Lord, You're our Father, our true Parent, no matter who our earthly mother and father may be," she prayed. "Help Parnell to see that, Lord. Please ease the pain this sudden discovery must have caused him."

Brenda sat quietly, trusting in God's sovereignty, and mulled over several of the many biblical promises she had committed to memory. Outside her living room window, the night was quiet, lit by a billion stars. Her physical hunger had abated and her spiritual focus seemed sharper. She was in a war, and she knew she possessed the winning weapon.

Forgiveness.

Parnell had been hurt, that went without saying. But she'd also been hurt—by the man who was supposed to love her. At the moment of crisis, when she needed him most, he'd checked out emotionally. Could she forgive Parnell for the grief he'd caused her? Could she love him unconditionally and not give in to the self-indulgence of holding a grudge? Could she? Did she want to?

Surely she had the right to a little self-pity? After the way he'd treated her? After his angry words?

Brenda listened to the wind moan around her house.

Forgive us our debts, as we forgive our debtors.

The verse came to mind with unmistakable clarity. She opened her eyes and put her Bible on the end table. She leaned forward, resting her elbows on her knees, entwining her fingers in a prayer-like position, holding them to her lips. Parnell had hurt her badly by his withdrawal, his anger and rejection. Even if she could forgive him, could she trust him again?

With God, nothing is impossible.

Brenda buried her face in her hands. Suddenly she saw that she needed to surrender her pride, her blithe confidence in her own ability to forgive. "Yes, Lord, of course You're right. I can't forgive Parnell, or anyone else, by myself. I need Your grace and Your mercy to be able to do that.

"Lord, take away my heart of stone and give me a heart of flesh. Write Your law of forgiveness on my heart. Help me let go of self-pity, nursing my wounds, brooding over insults. Help me be as generous as You were when You forgave your persecutors from the Cross. You chose to forgive them, Lord, just as You choose to forgive us. Lord, I want to forgive Parnell. Please give me the grace to do it."

Brenda had never before seen so clearly that forgiveness was a choice, an act of the will rather than emotion. All she had to offer God was her will, the area of life where He limits His divine sovereignty. She'd heard Pastor Milligan preach on the relationship between free will and forgiveness, but until this moment, the essential truths of what he'd said hadn't really come alive for her.

He'd preached the sermon weeks ago. Funny how she could recall it now, almost word for word. "Forgiveness, like love, is a conscious act," he'd said, his face earnest, his glasses halfway down his nose. "The memory of the wrong may come back, along with the human inclination to hold a grudge. But as creatures of free will, we can choose not to think about the wrongs we have suffered. Instead, we can work through the hurt, sometimes just by enduring it as Christ endured the pain of the cross. Forgiveness is an act of our will in obedience to the Lord."

Brenda felt her heart lightening. Her understanding quickened, as if someone had turned on a light in a dim room and she could see clearly objects that had only been fuzzy shapes before. So this was how the Holy Spirit enlightened one's mind. *By myself, Lord, I can do nothing. You're my only hope, Lord. Help me to remember that. I forget so easily.*

She closed her eyes. In her heart, she made the choice for love. As she did so, she felt the peace past understanding wrap her like sunlight engulfing a meadow on a summer morning. She relaxed, letting go of her sense of time and place. She allowed that timeless, placeless Presence to enfold her and seep into the depths of her being like the sun warming an old man's bones. She felt safe—loved.

Breathing deeply, she sat, content. With every breath she took in, she offered gratitude to her Creator for His amazing generosity, not only in answering her prayers, but in giving her life and then redeeming that life with His own. With every breath she exhaled, she gave Him back her life, with all its problems and joys, as a gift of trust.

After a while, she found herself thinking back to the conversation with her mother on Christmas Day. She could see how God had used her mother to help open her understanding. Yes, Louise had been right when she suggested Brenda's assumptions about Parnell were too limited. Now it seemed that even Parnell's assumptions about himself had been limited.

Why on earth had his parents hidden his adoption? Fergus Pierce was a well-respected minister. Why had they gone to such great lengths—changing Parnell's birth certificate? And how had Parnell found out? On the other hand, maybe it would help him be more understanding of why she'd given Emma up. A sudden stab of fear drove out that comforting thought. But what if it hardened him completely against adoption so that he'd push her even further away?

Brenda shivered. She couldn't bear for Parnell to shove her out of his life. Her longing for him was like a deep emptiness inside her. Her heart ached.

"Lord, I forgive Parnell. I'm trying to understand him, rather than just expecting him to understand me. But, Lord, even though You've given me this missing piece of the puzzle, I really have no assurance that Humpty Dumpty can be put together again. After all, Parnell has free will, too, and he can freely choose to reject me.

"O, Lord, You risked rejection—and received it—when You came to Your own and they turned You away. Freely-given love must be the most precious gift in the world for it to be worth such a terrible price. . ."

sixteen

Brenda snapped awake at the second ring of the telephone. As she groped in the dark for the telephone on the coffee table, she had the distinct impression that this call was the next step in God's unfolding plan.

She glanced over at the grandfather clock in the corner. By the light of the moon, she could make out the time. Eleven-thirty.

"Hello?"

"Brenda!"

She closed her eyes, inhaled deeply. Her grip on the receiver tightened. "Parnell, what is it?"

"It's Angelo. He's missing!"

"Missing? When? How?"

"He was upset when I put him to bed this evening. He was rambling on, something about you and the ducks. When I went in to check on him a few minutes ago, his bed was empty. He's not in the house. I've searched from top to bottom."

"Mrs. Crebs?"

"She's staying with her daughter for Christmas. Brenda, I'm sorry to call like this. . .after, well, after everything that's happened. It's just. . .well, you were the last person he talked about . . .how he missed you. Something about how you said you wouldn't leave him, like the ducks didn't leave."

A shaft of pain shot through Brenda's heart. Immediately, she knew where Angelo was. "Parnell, you know that small pond on your property? The one with the ducks? I think that's where he might have gone."

"I'll go there, right now."

"I'm on my way."

153

Brenda prayed all the way to Parnell's house, driving as fast as safety would allow. At least the roads were dry and clear. It hadn't snowed all day. But the cold was bone-chilling and Brenda pleaded for Angelo's safety, especially if he were out in this weather.

Ducks, dear Lord. He remembered the ducks. Lord, have mercy, protect Your child. Keep Angelo warm, Lord.

She parked along the curved drive in front of Parnell's mansion, flung herself out of the car, and ran across the yard toward the pond, which lay in a heavily wooded area about half a mile behind the house. Under the light of the full, pearl-white moon, the patches of snow left over from the Christmas Day storm radiated with an eerie, almost iridescent glow. The earth felt hard and frozen beneath her boots, and her breathlessness seemed to fill the whole night.

She caught sight of a tall, dark silhouette at the water's edge. A little bit behind Parnell, huge, old evergreen trees towered to cathedral heights. She redoubled her efforts and reached him just as he'd finished speaking into a cellular phone. A few mallards nodded along the frozen mud edging the pond.

"Parnell! Have you found him?"

One look at his grief-stricken face told her the answer. For a moment, she thought he was going to embrace her. He started to raise his arms, then dropped them by his side. Grimly, he looked across the lake. "No. I found a few spotty tracks leading down to the pond, but I haven't found him. I've just called the police."

Brenda steeled herself against the bitter cold. "Did he take his coat and hat?"

"Yes, at least that."

"I always harped on him to bundle up. . ."

"Yes. I did, too. . ." Parnell's voice trailed away in mute despair.

Brenda saw agony on his face as deep and desolate as the frozen landscape surrounding them. He stood ramrod straight, silent, his hand deep in the pockets of his overcoat, his shoulders hunched against the cold. He seemed to be a frozen incarnation of anguish, trapped in his inner isolation. Beyond the glassy lake, frozen drifts huddled up against the tool sheds and wooden fences surrounding the orchard of stark, barren apple trees.

Confronted with his distress, Brenda didn't know what to say.

At length, Parnell spoke. "Brenda, what have we done?" he cried, his voice breaking. He looked at her full in the face, his own contorting with grief.

"The ducks. . .the last time I took Angelo to the Pizza Palace, he asked me if I were really going to be his mother. I told him I was, and that just like the ducks who stay on the pond all winter, I wouldn't leave him."

"Oh, no!" Parnell covered his face with his hands and turned away. She wanted to reach out to him, to put her arms around him, but she restrained herself. For the sake of his dignity, she would leave initiation up to him.

For several moments, she watched his broad shoulders heave. Finally he said, without turning to her, "So this is what it feels like to lose a child. To have your heart ripped out of your chest, or your limbs hacked off."

"Yes, this is what it feels like. The pain lessens in time, but it never completely goes away."

"Before you gave your daughter up, did you know how much it would hurt?"

"I had a good idea."

"And you still gave her up?"

"Yes. Only because I thought it was best for her, like most every mother who makes that decision." *Lord, is this the time to tell him I know he's adopted? Or do I wait until he tells me?*

She had the distinct feeling she should wait. They stood in silence for several moments, listening to the wind whistling through the trees. Then Parnell cleared his throat. "So this is what my mother felt." His voice was a ragged whisper.

His words hung—jagged, cutting—on the cold air. She knew his heart must be raw and bleeding.

No clear thoughts filled Brenda's mind, but her soul cried out to God for wisdom. For a heartbeat, it seemed as though all of creation had stilled. Then she felt a soft whisper of wind against her face.

Suddenly, Brenda knew what to say, without hesitation or doubt. "Yes, Parnell. This is exactly what she felt. She suffered."

Parnell whirled around. He was staring at her as if he'd never seen her before. His dark eyes widened in disbelief. "You know?"

Brenda took a deep breath. "I found out earlier this evening when I went to see your grandmother. The young nurse there told me about your recent visit."

"You. . .you went to Pennsylvania? To the nursing home? Why?"

Brenda suppressed a smile of tenderness toward this man she loved so much. It was time to lay all her cards on the table, and take whatever came. "I went because I love you. I was searching for some clue that might explain why you were rejecting me. You wouldn't, or couldn't, tell me yourself, so I went on my own detective mission."

"Why?" he repeated, dumbstruck.

"I had to find out what was wrong, so our love could have another chance. I don't want to lose you, Parnell. I couldn't bear to go back to the loneliness of my life before you. Maybe I could learn to live without you, but I'd never be whole. I want to help you through this." She swallowed hard, and waited.

"It happened after the TV interview. . .with O'Reilly," Parnell began, his words tumbling out like water from a hose that had been stopped up. "My birth mother saw it and called me. She'd kept tabs on me through the newspaper stories about my work, but when she saw me humiliated on TV, she decided it was time to make contact. I never knew I was adopted, Brenda. Neither Fergus nor Janet ever told me. They even had my birth certificate changed!"

"Oh, Parnell!"

"Everything happened in one day. . . I'm sorry for pushing you away, for ignoring you at the very time you needed me most. I was hard-hearted and wrong, but. . ."

She nodded, understanding dawning like the sunrise. "It was all too much."

"Yes. At least, too much, too quickly. My anger. . .my remoteness. . .had more to do with my own confusion than with your giving up your child. After the initial shock wore off, I realized what a brave, unselfish thing you'd done. I was on my way to see you when the telephone call came that blew my orderly life to pieces, so. . .I never told you how much I admire the sacrifice you made for your daughter."

"Oh, Parnell. . .I love you so much. You don't know how good it is to hear you say you understand. It's worth all the hurt of these past few weeks. Have you met your birth mother?"

She saw the tremor cross his face. "No. . .not yet. I'm. . .I'm still recovering from the shock, I guess."

"I can't imagine how I'd feel if I suddenly discovered Louise wasn't my biological mother. You must be still reeling. But, I promise you this, Parnell, when you're ready—if you're ever ready—to meet her, I'll be there for you. We'll face it together."

A strand of blond hair blew across her face. He reached out his hand and swept it back with his fingertips. "You didn't give up on me. . .even when I was acting like a jerk. I'm so sorry," he said in a guttural whisper. "I've been such a fool."

In one quick movement, he enclosed her in his arms. "I don't deserve you. God knows, I don't. But if you'll still have me, I promise to love you for the rest of my life. . ."

Brenda closed her eyes and drank in the comfort of his embrace. *He who is forgiven much, loves much.* "Parnell, I'm sorry, too. I should have told you about Emma long ago. I'm sorry I gave you back your ring. I'm sorry I lashed out at you in anger. I. . ."

"Daddy! Brenda!" Angelo's small voice rang out. Brenda and Parnell sprang apart. Each spun around, searching for the direction of the voice. It seemed to come from one of the clusters of huge evergreen trees on the other side of the lake.

"Up here! In the big tree!"

"Thank God!" Parnell muttered as he sprinted toward the towering trees. He skirted the lake, which was about the size of a tennis court, with Brenda in close pursuit. Before she reached the trees, Parnell had already thrown off his coat and was scaling a broad trunk. "Hold on, son, I'm coming!" he yelled.

Brenda stood at the bottom of the tree and prayed that angels would surround these two men she loved more than life and keep them from falling.

"Angelo, hold onto my neck! There's a good boy! Hang on tight, just like I was giving you a piggyback ride, OK?"

"OK, Dad."

Parnell sounded worried to death; Angelo sounded, well, like a seven-year-old boy having a lark.

When Brenda saw his cold-reddened cheeks and nose, she supposed she should be stern, but instead she threw her arms around both Angelo and his father. "You had us so worried, Angelo! Angelo! Why did you run away?"

"I didn't run away! I just wanted to see the ducks, Brenda. To see if they really did stay all winter, like you said. Since you weren't gonna stay, I thought maybe they weren't gonna stay, either." Angelo frowned and tugged at his woolen cap, then hurried on. "Then I got cold, so I climbed the tree. Then I was too scared to climb down. Then I saw Dad and was afraid he'd be mad, 'cause he's been mad every day, but then you came and I knew everything would be all right."

"Oh, honey. . ." Brenda began.

She looked at Parnell and held her breath. For a moment, time seemed suspended. Then, in slow motion it seemed, Parnell reached up his hand and tenderly placed his palm against her cheek. "Things have changed, son," he said, looking at her but addressing his words to Angelo. "Brenda is staying. Aren't you, Brenda?"

Her throat closed with emotion. She grasped his hand and brought it to her lips, her kisses mingling with her tears. Finally, gazing into Parnell's face, but speaking to his son, she managed to get the words out. "Yes, Angelo. . .I'm staying. I promised I'd be you mommy, didn't I?"

"Cool!"

Parnell smiled slowly. "Cool!" he echoed.

"Yes, Parnell, I'm staying. Just try to make me leave."

His eyes, filled with more love than she'd ever seen, caressed her face. "You're mine," he said huskily. Then he looked down at his son and brushed a knuckle across Angelo's reddened cheek.

"And she's yours, too, son."

"That's right," said Brenda happily.

Angelo piped up. "Brenda, are you really gonna be my mommy now, for real?"

Gazing at Parnell's radiant face over Angelo's head, Brenda swallowed hard. "For real.".

"Oh, you guys are both my sweethearts!"

seventeen

Since Angelo's bedroom was directly above the kitchen, Brenda could hear Parnell's footsteps cross the room as he carried his exhausted son to bed. Poor Angelo. The child had nearly fallen asleep on Parnell's shoulder by the time they got back to the house and canceled the police call. He'd smiled when she'd kissed him on the cheek and told him good night.

It was a sleepy, secure smile that gave Brenda a warm feeling inside. Warm as fresh buttered toast, steaming cinnamon buns, hot chocolate by the fire on a winter's evening. Warm as. . .someone coming home, out of the cold.

Brenda stood with her hands on her hips surveying the kitchen and the adjoining living room she'd helped Parnell redecorate, bringing life and color to a house that had become an empty shell after Serena's death. Brenda knew this place so well. She belonged here.

Yes, she'd come home.

She sighed happily at the minor disaster she saw in the kitchen. She guessed it was due to Mrs. Crebs's Christmas vacation at her daughter's home. The good-natured, older woman acted as housekeeper, cook, and nanny for Parnell and Angelo. In her absence, it looked like Parnell had resorted to take-out food for practically every meal. Pizza boxes were piled in a leaning tower on the kitchen counter. Chinese cartons littered the table and sink. A couple of Taco Bell bags, stuffed with wrappers, lay on the floor beside the trash can. Empty Coke bottles and 7-Eleven coffee cups were scattered everywhere.

If ever there was a man who needs a wife, it's Parnell Pierce! Brenda grumbled to herself as she swept the empty cartons into the trash can and dumped the plastic bottles into the recycling bin. She wrung out a sponge in hot water and wiped down the counter and white, tile-topped kitchen table.

There! Now this place looks a little more like a home.

Marching over to the sunken living room—a study in masculine beiges and forest greens—Brenda plugged in the Christmas tree lights. The towering fir, a good ten feet high, was instantly transformed into a fairyland of white, blinking lights. Brenda guessed it was Mrs. Crebs herself who had trimmed the tree with red satin bows, white silk balls, Victorian lace hearts and cupid angels, and a graceful golden garland. Brenda stepped back and inhaled the fresh scent of pine, the smell of Christmas.

She and Parnell had missed Christmas Day, but maybe it wasn't too late to celebrate in their hearts. Moving quickly, before Parnell returned, Brenda flipped through his CD collection. She selected Handel's *Messiah,* the Westminster Boys' Choir singing Christmas favorites, and a selection of best-loved Christian hymns. She loaded them into the black plastic cartridge and pressed the button for random selection. Immediately, the soft strains of "Silent Night" filled the room with warmth and beauty.

The canary, Angelo's first veterinarian success, trilled along. Brenda skirted by the plethora of tall windows, each multi-paned and curtainless with only a green valance, and switched on the brass candles on each white window sill. Now, we're talking homey.

Briefly, she considered lighting the untouched log fire in the grate, but decided it would take too long to get a blaze going when she had more urgent needs to take care of. She'd suddenly realized how hungry she was. It was after midnight, and she'd had nothing but water and a few crackers all day. She hurried across the kitchen, threw open the refrigerator door, and dragged out sandwich fixings: rye bread, roast turkey sandwich meat, Swiss cheese, Dijon mustard, hot peppers, and mayonnaise, the kind with all the fat left in.

There's a time for fasting, and a time for feasting, she told herself as she smothered two slices of bread with mayonnaise. She piled on the meat, cheese, and pickles as she sang along with her favorite hymn, "Abide With Me," which the CD player had randomly selected.

"Abide with me, fast falls the eventide. . ."

She didn't notice Parnell until he'd sneaked up from behind and wrapped his arms around her. "Yes," he whispered, nuzzling her ear.

Brenda stopped her sandwich-making and leaned back into his strong embrace. "Yes, what?"

"Yes, I will 'abide with you.'"

"Oh!" She closed her eyes and relaxed, savoring his presence. "Promise?"

"Yes, I promise. I promise to abide with you, to treasure you, to spend my life making up for the hurt I've caused you."

Brenda placed her hand over his, running her fingertips across the warm skin. "You've given us another chance, that's enough," she said. "Now I know you love me, in good times and in bad."

"What else can I do?"

"We need to talk," she said, pulling away a little. "I need to know why this happened. . .and I need to eat.

Parnell released her and leaned up against the counter, arms folded, studying her face. "You look tired, pale. . .wan, even. Are you feeling OK?"

"Just hungry, I guess," Brenda said quickly as she spread a thin layer of Dijon mustard on top of the Swiss cheese and closed the sandwich.

"So, you're not sick?"

"No, I just haven't eaten all day."

Parnell's eyes narrowed, accenting the deep lines in his face. "You're not dieting, are you? Your figure is perfect as it is, you know."

Brenda chuckled as she picked up her plate and moved over to the table. "No, I'm not dieting, and thanks for the compliment. I was just. . .skipping meals." Suddenly she found herself in an awkward situation. She didn't want to disclose her fasting, which she knew was meant to be kept a discreet part of a Christian's spiritual walk. But neither did she want to lie nor keep secrets from Parnell. *No more secrets. So here goes, Lord. You know I'm not bragging.*

"Well, actually. . .I was fasting today."

"Fasting? Why?" Parnell's eyes opened wide.

"For you. For us. As part of my campaign as a prayer warrior." She flashed him a practical, no-nonsense smile as she bit into her thick sandwich.

Parnell's eyebrows shot up. Quickly, he sat down, scraping the legs of his chair across the tiles. "Fasting? For me? Oh, Brenda!"

"Nothing's too much trouble for the man I love," she said between mouthfuls, thoroughly enjoying both the meal and the look of surprised delight flooding Parnell's handsome features. He looked deeply touched.

"Sweetheart, I don't know what to say. I'm speechless. Flabbergasted. Honored."

"How about getting me some lemonade?"

"Anything your little heart desires, my lady love. Would you like potato chips as well?"

Brenda grinned. "You bet."

Parnell rose, and bowed from his waist. "Barbecue or sour cream, m'lady?"

"Oh, barbecue will do nicely."

Parnell pulled a canister of Mr. Pringle out of the white cupboards lining the wall. Snapping off the aluminum seal, he poured the chips into a glass bowl and set them beside Brenda. "No roses tonight," he said. "No fancy seafood dinner. Only barbecue chips, turkey and Swiss sandwiches. . .and my heart."

He smiled and Brenda melted.

Striding over to the refrigerator, he retrieved a can of lemonade.

"A glass for m'lady?"

"I should jolly well think so, Jeeves. What kind of a lady do you think I am, drinking out of a can like a commoner? Off with your head!" She waved her hand in a sweeping motion.

Parnell laughed, his dark eyes twinkling. "Oh, Brenda, it's good to have you back. Life is so. . .dull without you." He poured the lemonade into a clear glass and handed it to Brenda, briefly touching her hand. "Not to mention lonely."

"I know. I've missed you, too." Brenda took a sip of her lemonade. "Very nice lemonade, if I do say so myself."

Parnell shook his head. "You've been watching too many British dramas on public television."

"Maybe," she conceded her one television vice. "But, talking about drama, sit down and tell me the whole story of how your birth mother contacted you. I want to know everything. No more secrets."

Parnell sat down heavily and propped his elbows on the tiled table top. He took a chip and began fiddling with it, turning it over and over. "It's hard to know where to begin," he finally admitted, biting into the chip.

"Sometimes it helps just to begin," said Brenda, remembering her mother's advice. "Just jump in anywhere."

"The telephone call," said Parnell, running his hand across his trimmed beard. "I think that's when my emotional circuit board overloaded."

"She didn't call until after the O'Reilly fiasco?"

Parnell pressed his lips together. "That's right. You see, Brenda, given a little time to recover from O'Reilly's shell shock, I could have handled the news of…Emma…with more grace."

Brenda breathed sharply. He said the name with such tenderness, as if her longlost daughter had become a real person to him, not just an embarrassing secret. "Go on," she whispered.

"After I dropped you off, I drove around for a couple of hours. Drove all the way to downtown Washington, D.C., as a matter of fact. I walked around aimlessly. After a while, I figured out what had happened. You'd been building up to tell me, but O'Reilly beat you to the punch."

Brenda nodded. *Thank You, Lord. He understands!*

"I was going to call you as soon as I got home. In fact, I'd just walked into the house when she called." Parnell stopped and hauled in a deep breath, as if fortifying himself. "Her name, I mean, my birth mother's name is Dolores Currano. At first I thought it was a prank call, but there was something about her voice. She sounded sincere. She said she finally called because she'd seen O'Reilly's spot on TV, and she was worried for me."

Brenda smiled, figuring that if she'd been in Dolores Currano's shoes, she'd have been worried, too. "Go on," she said.

"Well, the more she talked, the more I believed she was for real. She explained that she'd been a frightened, pregnant teenager in Annapolis, the same town where my father was in the seminary and my mother worked as a nurse to support him."

"Dolores Currano," echoed Brenda, wiping her hands on a paper napkin. "Sounds Italian."

"Yep. Explains the black hair and tan, doesn't it?"

Brenda smiled and took another sip of lemonade. The food had revived her and she sat in rapt attention as Parnell went on with the story.

"Seems my mother was a cheerleader at her high school and my father was a football jock. She turned up pregnant after homecoming. He pressured her to get an illegal abortion—this was pre-1972 and Roe vs. Wade—but before he could make arrangements, a fellow cheerleader persuaded Dolores to speak to a Christian nurse. Deep down, Dolores, my mother, wanted to be talked out of an abortion. Janet Pierce was only too happy to do the talking."

Brenda gaped. "Wow! So..."

Parnell was on a roll. "So Janet, who couldn't have children because of an emergency hysterectomy before she met Fergus, agreed to take me. More like she begged and pleaded. Dolores lived with Janet and Fergus for the rest of her pregnancy and they paid all her medical costs."

Brenda shook her head, remembering her own pregnancy. She found her eyes filling with tears at the providence of God that visited Dolores Currano through the kindness of strangers.

"My mother—I mean, Janet—shared her faith, and Dolores came to know the Lord. Dolores told me she prayed a lot when she was carrying me. She believed that giving me up was the right thing, and that gave her some comfort. After my birth,

Dolores moved back home and eventually went to college. She believed it would be better for me not to know her, so she purposely didn't contact the Pierces. But when I was older, she kept track of me and my career from afar."

Brenda cleared her throat and tilted her head to one side. "And the birth certificate?"

"Fergus and Janet had it legally changed. They didn't want anyone, including me, apparently, to know I wasn't theirs. I can only speculate that they, or maybe it was mostly Janet, wanted a child so badly that they couldn't admit I wasn't their natural child."

Brenda took a sip of lemonade. "How do you feel about Janet and Fergus keeping this secret?"

Parnell caught and held her gaze. "I'll admit I was angry, at first. Furious, even. I think that was mostly shock, though. Kind of like the automatic angry response you get when someone cuts you off in traffic. Or maybe a more suitable analogy is if someone pulled a rug out from under your feet."

"And so you clammed up," Brenda added.

Parnell shrugged. "Yep. Sure did. I guess I thought if I didn't talk about it. . .it might go away. Denial, huh?"

Brenda nibbled on a potato chip and nodded.

"But now I see that I was grieving, and taking it out on you." His gaze moved over her face in a gentle caress. "I'm sorry."

A smile began in Brenda's heart and spread to her lips. "You're forgiven."

"You see, Janet was adopted," Parnell went on.

"I think I remember your mentioning that once."

"If I did, it was only in passing. You see, it wasn't discussed in our house. Janet's mother never let her forget she was an illegitimate, adopted child who owed her something."

"Oh, Parnell, how awful for Janet! No wonder she didn't want to pass on an adoption legacy to you! Now this is beginning to make more sense."

Parnell grimaced. "Janet not only had a lousy experience with her own adoption, but she also suffered from depression because she couldn't have children of her own. Nobody in Dad's congregation knew it, but Janet was hospitalized for depression twice. She was fragile, emotionally. Maybe she wanted a child so badly, it was easy to pretend I was hers. And I was hers, in every way that counted. She was a wonderful mother.

"And I can see Fergus's point of view, too. He was shielding the woman he'd vowed to love and protect. They moved to a new church in Baltimore shortly after they adopted me. It must have been the easiest thing in the world just to let people think I was their natural child. I even had dark hair, like Fergus."

Brenda nodded. "Yes, that would have been easy."

"And understandable. Fergus loved Janet very much," said Parnell after a second's hesitation. "Maybe he was afraid that telling would push her into another depression. How can I not forgive them, Brenda? What they did was wrong, yes, but they were also doing the best they could. I don't believe for a moment that they actually meant to hurt me."

Parnell rose, strolled over to the refrigerator, and got himself a lemonade. He popped the tab and drank out of the can as he stood in front of the kitchen sink, staring out at the clear, chaste stars set like diamonds in black velvet. He sighed deeply. "To get on with the story. At college, Dolores met a good man who was studying to be a doctor. Eventually they married and settled down in a suburb of Annapolis. He practiced medicine and they had six children, all boys. Can you imagine, Brenda? I—a lonely, only child—have six half-brothers! But even with all those children, Dolores says she never forgot me and always prayed for me."

Brenda swallowed the lump in her throat as she studied Parnell's solemn profile. What must it be like for him to find this out, after all these years? *Dear Lord, give him strength.*

Parnell turned and looked at her, a piercing, searing look. "Do you know what Dolores did after her boys were older?"

"Tell me."

"She became a pro-life lobbyist in the state capitol."

Brenda sat quietly, marveling at the intricate weaving of God's handiwork in their lives.

"She heard about my parents' deaths on the news, and she

followed the legal fiasco with the Montgomery clan. She ached
for me, she said. Prayed for me constantly. Several times she
nearly made contact. But she didn't. She didn't know if I knew
I'd been adopted."

Brenda swallowed hard. "So it was O'Reilly's meanness that
tipped her hand?"

"Yes. Can you believe that? She knows the media pretty well,
and she could tell we'd been set up. She wanted to offer her support and comfort. Do you know what she told me about you?"

Brenda's eyes opened wide. She shook her head.

"She said, 'Don't be too hard on that girl. She's been through
hell. She's never forgotten that baby.' I gather she was speaking
from personal experience?"

Brenda's gaze fell to her hands in her lap. "Yes," she said softly.

Parnell's voice grew tender. "It wasn't just the shock of finding out I had a mother I never knew about. I also discovered I
could have been aborted. I've had to do a lot of soul-searching,
Brenda. Do you remember I told you that I believed abortion was
a matter of choice, perhaps the lesser of two evils? I was wrong,
Brenda, so wrong. It must have felt like a slap in the face to hear
me dismiss abortion so easily when you'd suffered so much to do
the right thing. But until Dolores called, abortion was an ab-
stract issue for me. Then, suddenly, it had a face—my face, and
by extension, Angelo's face."

Parnell put his drink on the counter and closed the distance
between them in three long strides. He stood across the table
from Brenda, his hands planted on the table, his body leaning
toward her. She saw the urgency slashed across his features.
"Dolores said she doesn't know what she would have done if abortion had been legal back then. She doesn't know if she would
have been strong enough to withstand the pressure to take the
easy way out."

He lowered his voice and spoke with great feeling. "Brenda,
I'm probably alive because the Roe vs. Wade lawsuit hadn't come
to court yet."

Brenda nodded, taking in his seriousness. "You're probably

right. It doesn't make sense, does it?"

"No! It's insane! Why do I get to live, but not the millions of babies who were conceived and then legally terminated after Roe vs. Wade? Just lucky timing? The right to life shouldn't be based on luck, or convenience, or whim, or even a legal ruling. Life is life."

Suddenly, he grabbed Brenda's hand and pulled her to her feet. He looked intently into her eyes. "Thank you for being strong enough to give your child the gift of life," he said. "I'm just sorry I haven't said this to you before. If I have any excuse, it's that I was on an emotional overload and my circuits blew. . .and you, my love," he raised her hand and kissed it, "were the unfortunate victim of the fallout.

"I tried to tell you," Parnell continued, his breath warm against her hand. "I wanted to, but I froze up every time."

Brenda reached up and cupped the side of his face. "I understand. Don't be too hard on yourself, Parnell. You're only human."

Parnell pulled her to his chest. She buried her face in the softness of his sweater. "Brenda, I've been blessed. I'm a rich man. I want to start doing something to help women choose life. It seems to me that many mothers, if they were given the practical help they needed, would choose to give their babies a chance."

Brenda wrapped her arms around Parnell, hugging him, feeling safe and secure. "I think most women choose abortion like an animal chooses to chew off its leg to escape a trap. It's desperation, not choice. Take Rita Andreas, for instance. . ."

Parnell stiffened. "Rita? Reggie? You're not saying. . ."

"I'm afraid so. She's pregnant, and it looks like Reggie's exercising his freedom of choice by opting for his music career over his responsibilities. Rita's scared stiff. I've promised her she'll always have her job with me, but she's so worried about her apartment. . ."

Parnell slid his hands down Brenda's arms and gently moved her away from him, holding her at arms' length. Excitement danced across his face. "Once we're married and you become the mistress of my humble abode, you won't need your house on Thunder Hill anymore, right?"

Brenda nodded, wondering where this was leading.

"OK, so we pay off your mortgage and sign the house over to Rita—on one condition."

Brenda's eyes opened wide. "What condition?"

"That she takes in another woman in a crisis pregnancy, to help that mother-to-be along the way. And when the woman moves on, that she takes in another, and so on. This could be the start of a whole new housing ministry! Maybe we could even get Dolores involved. . ."

Brenda smiled, thrilled at Parnell's enthusiasm. "Parnell, I think that's the most wonderful idea I've heard since you declared your intention to 'abide' with me."

Parnell traced the shape of her face with his thumb. "Abide with me, for better or for worse, my love. We've been through some of the worse. . .are you ready for the better?"

"More than ready!"

A Letter To Our Readers

Dear Reader:

In order that we might better contribute to your reading enjoyment, we would appreciate your taking a few minutes to respond to the following questions. When completed, please return to the following:

Rebecca Germany, Managing Editor
Heartsong Presents
P.O. Box 719
Uhrichsville, Ohio 44683

1. Did you enjoy reading *Abide With Me*?
   ❑ Very much. I would like to see more books
      by this author!
   ❑ Moderately
      I would have enjoyed it more if _____
      _____

2. Are you a member of **Heartsong Presents**? ❑Yes ❑No
   If no, where did you purchase this book?_____
   _____

3. What influenced your decision to purchase this
   book? (Check those that apply.)

   ❑ Cover   ❑ Back cover copy

   ❑ Title   ❑ Friends

   ❑ Publicity   ❑ Other_____

4. How would you rate, on a scale from 1 (poor) to 5
   (superior), the cover design?_____

5. On a scale from 1 (poor) to 10 (superior), please rate the following elements.

___Heroine   ___Plot

___ Hero   ___ Inspirational theme

___ Setting   ___Secondary characters

6. What settings would you like to see covered in **Heartsong Presents** books?_____

_____

_____

7. What are some inspirational themes you would like to see treated in future books?_____

_____

_____

8. Would you be interested in reading other **Heartsong Presents** titles?   ❏ Yes   ❏ No

9. Please check your age range:
   ❏ Under 18   ❏ 18-24   ❏ 25-34
   ❏ 35-45   ❏ 46-55   ❏ Over 55

10. How many hours per week do you read? _____

Name _____

Occupation _____

Address _____

City_____ State_____ Zip _____

Heartsong Presents Classics!

We have put together a collection of some of the most popular **Heartsong Presents** titles in two value-priced volumes. Favorite titles from our first year of publication, no longer published in single volumes, are now available in our new *Inspirational Romance Readers*.

___**Historical Collection #1** includes: *A Torch for Trinity* by Colleen L. Reece; *Whispers on the Wind* by Maryn Langer; *Cottonwood Dreams* by Norene Morris; and *A Place to Belong* by Tracie J. Peterson (originally written under the pen name Janelle Jamison).

___**Contemporary Collection #1** includes: *Heartstrings* by Irene B. Brand; *Restore the Joy* by Sara Mitchell; *Passage of the Heart* by Kjersti Hoff Baez; and *A Matter of Choice* by Susannah Hayden.

Each collection is $4.97 each plus $1.00 for shipping and handling. Buy both collections for $8.99 plus $1.00 for shipping and handling.

Hearts♥ng Presents
Love Stories Are Rated G!

That's for godly, gratifying, and of course, great! If you love a thrilling love story, but don't appreciate the sordidness of some popular paperback romances, **Heartsong Presents** is for you. In fact, **Heartsong Presents** is the *only inspirational romance book club*, the only one featuring love stories where Christian faith is the primary ingredient in a marriage relationship.

Sign up today to receive your first set of four, never before published Christian romances. Send no money now; you will receive a bill with the first shipment. You may cancel at any time without obligation, and if you aren't completely satisfied with any selection, you may return the books for an immediate refund!

Imagine. . .four new romances every four weeks—two historical, two contemporary—with men and women like you who long to meet the one God has chosen as the love of their lives. . .all for the low price of $9.97 postpaid.

To join, simply complete the coupon below and mail to the address provided. **Heartsong Presents** romances are rated G for another reason: They'll arrive *Godspeed!*